JAMES PATTERSON is one of the best-known and biggest-selling writers of all time. His books have sold in excess of 325 million copies worldwide and he has been the most borrowed author in UK libraries for the past nine years in a row. He is the author of some of the most popular series of the past two decades – the Alex Cross, Women's Murder Club, Detective Michael Bennett and Private novels – and he has written many other number one bestsellers including romance novels and stand-alone thrillers.

James is passionate about encouraging children to read. Inspired by his own son who was a reluctant reader, he also writes a range of books for young readers including the Middle School, I Funny, Treasure Hunters, House of Robots, Confessions and Maximum Ride series. James is the proud sponsor of the World Book Day Award and has donated millions in grants to independent bookshops. He lives in Florida with his wife and son.

BOOK**SHOTS**

STORIES AT THE SPEED OF LIFE

What you are holding in your hands right now is no ordinary book, it's a BookShot.

BookShots are page-turning stories by James Patterson and other writers that can be read in one sitting.

Each and every one is fast-paced, 100% story-driven; a shot of pure entertainment guaranteed to satisfy.

Available as new, compact paperbacks, ebooks and audio, everywhere books are sold.

BookShots – the ultimate form of storytelling. From the ultimate storyteller.

JAMES
PATTERSON

WITH SHAN SERAFIN

BOOKSHOTS

3 5 7 9 10 8 6 4 2

BookShots
20 Vauxhall Bridge Road
London SW1V 2SA

BookShots is part of the Penguin Random House group of companies whose addresses can be found at global.penguinrandomhouse.com.

First published by BookShots in 2016

www.penguin.co.uk

A CIP catalogue record for this book is available from the British Library.

ISBN 9781786530851

Printed and bound in Great Britain by Clays Ltd, St Ives Plc

COME AND GET US

CHAPTER 1

I HAD NO way of knowing it at the time, but when Aaron told his joke, I was thirty-nine seconds away from driving our minivan through a guardrail over a cliff and into a river. I would be steering us down a canyon, bringing the two people in this world I care about most to the brink of death.

And somehow, that wasn't the worst thing that happened that afternoon.

This is what happened.

We were driving down a desolate stretch of highway. Three of us. Me, my husband, Aaron, and my daughter, Sierra. We were in the gorgeous no-man's land between Utah and Arizona, a few canyons north of the "grand" one. Normally, I'm chatty behind the wheel, trading terrible jokes and bad puns with Aaron, but roads like these leave no margin for error.

"What do you say if you meet a talking duck and an honest lawyer?" he asked.

When a car is speeding along a curvy highway and starts to lose traction near the edge of a cliff, the solution, believe it or not, is to turn *toward* the direction of the skid. This means toward the cliff, toward the unthinkable. It sounds logical from a physics perspective. Turning into a skid. It sounds like the sort of level-headed action that everyone at a cocktail party would nod in agreement about. *Yes, do that. Steer toward the tragedy. We'd all do that obvious, logical thing.*

Thirty-one seconds.

But what if the reason you're skidding in the first place isn't simply because you lost focus but because a three-ton black SUV has intentionally sent you into it?

There was an SUV behind us.

Inches behind us. Its menacing grill was flooding my rearview mirror, looking like Darth Vader's helmet on wheels. The driver—fat, bearded, and ugly—was coming as close as possible to touching my minivan's rear.

"Let him think he's winning," said Aaron, calmly backseat-driving me.

He was next to our four-year-old, helping her command the galactic kangaroos in her video game.

"Let him think he's winning?" I replied. *"Why?"*

Sierra had recently reached what many parents herald as the new milestone in child development: how to complain about the wifi signal she needed to upgrade the game. But Aaron was her voice of reason. And mine.

I knew what he was getting at—I should calmly drift over and give the tailgater enough room to split our lane, so that he could pass us and be on his angry little way.

"I don't want to pull over for him," I said. "I don't want to reward that kind of behavior."

"He's a grown man, not a Labrador."

I took a breath, a yogic breath. "Fine. What *do* you say if you meet a talking duck and an honest lawyer?"

"Holy crap, an honest lawyer!" said Aaron, which made him laugh.

I slowed down and drifted. He was right. I was letting a trivial situation get the best of me. Time to be the adult and let it go.

I took my foot off the gas a smidgen and sure enough, my new friend came up alongside my left fender, trading his monopoly of my rearview mirror for a monopoly of the side one. I'd already prepared the perfect facial expression for him, a mix of disdain and tranquility.

But he kept that satisfaction from me.

He hovered in my blind spot, then decisively faded back into his original position.

Seventeen seconds. I immediately glanced ahead on the highway, thinking he'd seen something in front of us. Construction cones? A bridge? Trucks? But we were the only two cars out here, traveling together through the desolate desert cliffs. Before he pulled up behind us moments ago, we hadn't seen another car for an hour.

"He's not passing us," I informed Aaron.

"Good. See? Zen," he replied. "Let him *think* he has the power and, presto, the guy retreats."

Mr. SUV had indeed faded back to my rear but he was still following close behind. Close, until three seconds later he was trying to pass me again but on the opposite side now, on the shoulder side of the road. This put him on the inner path of a very blind turn. Let him fly by, I mused to myself. Good riddance.

Eight seconds.

The healthy thought didn't dispel the rising tension I was feeling.

"Sierra, hold my paw," said Aaron to our daughter. That was their little code for assurance—whenever there was a goblin in the house or a clap of thunder in the distance, the two koalas in the family held tight.

"Daddy, hold my paw," she immediately echoed back. Five seconds.

Sensing the tension in the car, they were now entwined. Just in time. The SUV was *so* close to us—when it happened.

He clipped the far corner of my rear bumper, a solid enough strike but not nearly hard enough to seem like anything other than an accident. I lost control of our car. Four seconds.

We began to skid clockwise, toward the guardrail.

Two-point-five seconds.

And instead of flashing on the cocktail party in Manhattan when we'd joked about how to react in a high-speed car chase—three years ago, when Aaron got hired for his first big job as a lawyer, for a nice corporation called Drake Oil—I instead flashed on the general concept of my husband and Sierra in my backseat, innocently playing together in the kangaroo galaxy.

And I hesitated at the wheel.

There was no time anyway.

Seventy-three miles per hour.

We were going to go over the edge.

Zero.

CHAPTER 2

I HIT THE guardrail at over seventy miles an hour, exploding the metal post from its anchor in the rock and shattering the metal outward as if it were the fringes of a ribbon, at the end of a marathon.

My heart froze, not just for what was happening in the moment, but for what was looming ahead on my disturbingly clear horizon.

There was no ground in sight.

We were going over a cliff.

It was just air meeting dashboard. There was no ground in this picture.

"Miranda!" my husband screamed, the involuntary expulsion of your wife's name when terror takes hold of your vocal cords.

The front of the minivan flew forward as my stomach sank about ten miles below my seat. All four tires went airborne as 99 percent of the ambient noise abruptly vanished, like someone clicked off the master volume on life, which, in turn, ushered in the horrific sound of my four-year-old daughter screaming at the top of her lungs. The most bloodcurdling, most agonized shriek imaginable.

"Mmmmaaaaammmmaaa*aaaa!*"

My entire body went rigid as my inner organs twisted in a knot. I stomped my foot down on the brake pedal, crushing it into the floor, as if brakes mattered while our minivan did what minivans were not supposed to do.

We were airborne and then, we were not. We rejoined the planet without slowing down at all. The front of the van hit the dirt, a massive grade leading toward the abyss. We flipped over, for a second on all four wheels, and I felt the traction of the tires bite for just a second as I had a chance to correct the careening vehicle ever-so-slightly forward again.

It was a brief moment of hope, but there was no control. Our minivan kept flipping, vertically and horizontally.

As the world spun in front of me, I caught a glimpse in the rearview mirror of my treasures—screaming and crying just as I must have been. We bounced horrendously along the spine of the hillside with its rocky dirt hammering our tires and our chassis, until we finally smashed into the bottom of the canyon.

Upside down.

Where everything then became eerily still. Everyone's cries had stopped.

Only the river murmured. It was getting in somehow, trickling across our ceiling. We were partially on the rapids, partially on the shallow end of the bank.

Only later would I appreciate that while bad luck had delivered me an SUV to contend with, good luck had delivered me the one spot by the river that would hold us. A dozen feet farther and we'd be submerged.

I turned to look behind me. I saw my husband, seemingly drifting in and out of consciousness.

"You good?" I asked him.

He didn't look good. It took him a long moment to answer. "Mmmmm…"

"Sierra?" I said to my daughter, a one-word query.

She was wide-eyed but alert, apparently intact.

I instantly activated myself. Sleeves rolled up. Time to move. All of us. My husband, though sluggish, started fiddling with the straps on Sierra's car seat. I took off my seat belt, trying to land as gracefully as possible onto the wet ceiling. It wasn't very graceful. I looked back to Aaron to make sure he and Sierra could both wiggle free. His forehead had a nasty gash across it. Long, thick, deep. But he was present enough to help Sierra down.

"I'm gonna climb back up to the main road," I announced to him.

" 'Kay," he replied.

I'd fully expected him to debate me, to tell me he should be the one to go, to tell me I should stay here with Sierra, but he didn't protest. I wasn't sure if that was a good thing or a bad thing.

I didn't dwell on it. I got moving. The shock neutralized any hesitation I might have had, maybe should have. I was numbly executing a series of actions I wasn't even sure would work. We needed help, serious help. An ambulance. A medical helicopter. We hadn't had reception for a long time, and I couldn't see either of our phones, which must have bounced around the van.

Water was really starting to get in, now—I realized that most of the windows were shattered. Of course they were.

One thing went right, though: I had no idea what inconvenient place we decided to cram our emergency kit when we packed the car, but there it was, in the middle of all our other belongings, on the ceiling, getting wet. I grabbed it and slung it on my shoulder like a purse.

I kicked out the shattered glass of the passenger window—luckily the van was in at an angle, and the passenger's side was slightly above the water.

Even though the SUV driver had just shoved me off

the road, I somehow expected him to be yelling down to us right now, to have realized what he'd done, pulled over, and formulated a plan for getting help down here to us.

But I'd seen enough cop shows that I realized what had happened up on the road wasn't accidental. It was called the PIT maneuver.

And he'd run us off intentionally.

CHAPTER 3

WHEN I GOT out I looked up and saw that the rock face was much steeper than I anticipated. A vintage Grand Canyon-y type of cliff face. The whole region looked like a slice of Mars with an extra sprinkling of jagged cliffs. I wasn't really sure how Sierra was going to get up there, let alone my injured husband. Frankly, I wasn't even sure how *I* was going to get up.

It would be a grueling climb—maybe better described as a scramble, though the more I considered the angle, it looked like a downright free climb. This wasn't totally daunting: I was once a strong climber, even competitive; but that was years ago. My exercise regimen these days was mainly chasing a toddler around the house.

Nowhere to go but up, though, if I were going to flag down help on the road. I hoped for muscle memory when the time came. Is climbing a rock face like riding a bike?

I was snapped out of my assessment of the rock face when I heard a groan. The minivan was moving. The river was *moving* the minivan!

It should have been safe in the shallows. It wasn't.

"Aaron, the van's moving!" I shouted.

I ducked back into the passenger window I had kicked out to find Aaron stuck in the backseat, pinned by the vehicle's journey into the silt. The passenger seat had broken and had buckled onto his thigh.

He tried to hand me Sierra, but she refused to leave him. She was huddled behind the driver's seat, now half-way deep in river water.

Despite her panic and his head wound, he remained calm and managed to pick her up and tried to hand her to me.

But there was nowhere to go. The path I'd waded through the current was a one-way street too turbulent to retreat against. We coaxed her out through the front passenger window, but there was nowhere to set her down—I wasn't going to put my four-year-old in running river water.

I managed to open the sliding rear door enough for him to fit through, and began to pull on him, one arm holding Sierra, one arm pulling Aaron. He was using one free hand to push himself and the other to push on the broken seat pinning him. The car was tilting toward the river now. I didn't realize how precariously we were balanced but we didn't have much time. Aaron was frantically trying to extricate his leg.

"On the count of three," I said. "One…two…"

"Three," we both grunted. And pried him free.

We were waist deep when the van flipped into the water, submerging the top half. We stared for a moment at what would have been our family coffin. We'd gotten out on the far side of the river, on the wrong side to go back to the road. Aaron started moving across it, his head bleeding. I didn't know how he was functioning. I followed, clutching our daughter. The current quickly became brutal, but the three of us kept trudging along. We were now chest-deep in the rapids, water gushing past us at a relentless velocity. But we could see the direct route to the nearest bank, and it didn't seem to be getting any deeper. The hard part was over.

And then I lost my grip on Sierra.

"Aaron!" I screamed. She was already six feet away from my outstretched hand. *"Aaron!"* I needed him to turn around and outstretch his.

He looked back and instantly lunged to grab her—thank God—by the arm. And held tight. But he'd lunged downstream, and lost his balance. And they were now being carried away. Fast. All I could see was the top of her purple Kangaroo Commander hat bobbing downstream.

I got to the bank of dirt and rocks and ran helplessly alongside the buoyant duo. Everything in the world I cared about was floating twenty feet away from me amid raging rapids, soon to be squirted between the jagged rock-teeth of the river.

If I could get ahead, I could start thinking about sliding down the bank to water level and extending myself across the rocks to grab them. But the current was increasing—*where is it taking them?* I ran along the bank and began to see and hear what had seemed faraway before: there was a waterfall ahead. Of course.

CHAPTER 4

I'D BEEN RUNNING blind. I hadn't paid attention to the horizon. Sierra and Aaron were about to go over the edge. *Haven't we had enough edges today?* I lost my footing for a step as I opened up my stride, but managed to stay on pace, sprinting along with them.

"The branches!" yelled my husband.

"What?" I yelled back.

It took me a moment to realize he meant the lone tree growing out of the rocky bank, way up on the left side, imprisoned by the relentless current. My mind raced. Okay, all I have to do is race ahead, hop down along the wet, slippery stones, grab at the trunk, break off a branch, hope it was the right length, hope it was the right sturdiness, then dangle it out across Aaron's path.

Sierra looked too shocked to be scared. She was clamping onto his neck while he was trying to hold her up and protect her from the hidden rocks. He was on his back, traveling legs first so his feet could absorb a blow if a rock or tree trunk surfaced; cupping her on his torso like an otter might shield its treasure.

"Hold a branch across," he shouted.

I knew what to do and had very little time to do it. I was racing down toward the tree.

I'd finally surpassed them in the race. Now, with a little bit of a lead, I'd have a moment to turn toward the water and hustle over to the tree and break off the best possible—

I was too late.

They went over the falls before I could even complete my yell. "Aaron!" I cried. The involuntary expulsion of your husband's name.

I thought I could get to them in time but I didn't anticipate just how much the current would accelerate near the drop. They simply disappeared over the edge. Followed by my useless shouts.

"Aaron!"

It was as if they had been yanked below a horizontal line of existence. I was so shocked by what I saw that I halted in my tracks, struggling to maintain any rational grasp on the situation.

Within a moment, I snapped back into awareness and resumed the chase to see where they had landed. I arrived at the edge on the left bank and searched the river below. It was as large a waterfall as I'd feared, with one factor in our favor: the plunge pool wasn't rocky. There was enough clear depth down there to accommodate a full drop. Within several torturous seconds I saw them, two heads bobbing along. They'd survived.

In a wider section of the river, with only slow rapids, they were floating in a froth that lasted maybe five seconds before pushing its fresh contents downstream. I scurried down the wet crags and was soon keeping up with them along the gentle current. They were thankfully moving much slower now.

"She's okay," Aaron shouted to me.

I skidded on my butt down a rocky, dirty incline. He pulled himself onto the bank just as I arrived. Sierra was wide-eyed, frozen in fear. She wasn't speaking.

He handed her to me so that he could finally collapse. I hugged them both, embracing their icy skin. He looked ready to pass out, but I didn't feel good about him surrendering consciousness.

"Not here, babe," I said.

He was ghostly pale from a loss of blood and from the water. The air was warm, but the water was cold. And he'd pushed himself through the entire ordeal running on fumes, on adrenaline.

"Let's get over to those crags," I said to him. "See? Down by that first boulder?"

He didn't answer.

"Babe?" I said to him, waiting for him to find the strength to speak.

"Crags," he finally replied, deflating.

I looked at Sierra. She still seemed shell-shocked, but physically unscathed. "You okay?" I asked her.

"Crags," she agreed. My cooperative tag team.

I grabbed my husband by the hand and helped him up. We thus began the four-legged, three-person limp toward the boulders looming nearby. I'd also spotted some cavelike openings, amid the spill of giant rock fragments. We could hide in one of those. This would be important—to keep us out of the direct sun, away from animals, away from wind, and away from the cold of night, if we were still here then.

It's important, when taking refuge, to make sure someone knows your chosen locale. We did have a signal flare in the emergency kit I had grabbed. It had a granola bar, a magnifying glass, a first aid kit, a canteen, and the flare. And I'd glimpsed what I thought was a small town in the distance while running along the river. It was far away, but I had to assume it would have a few residents who might be looking in our direction.

"I think we should send up the flare," I said to him.

He could barely keep his eyes open.

"Or should we wait?" I asked.

He was too weary but found enough determination

to give me a meek thumbs-up before fading again. I had no idea if that thumb meant *yes, wait,* or *yes, send it*.

"Uh," I said. "Did...?"

So I sent it.

PFFFFFaaaaffff! The colorful firework popped in the sky about five hundred feet above us. Sierra was in awe. Aaron barely noticed. I hated to do this in broad daylight, but nightfall might be longer than we could wait.

Once inside the cave, my husband collapsed on the dirt. I'd intended to find a good spot for him, but gravity had made that decision for us and I didn't have the heart to move him.

"This'll work," I said.

I started to lecture him about the importance of elevating the wound. He had a gash on his forehead, and its flow needed stanching. But after five sentences of lecturing, I realized he was out cold. Sierra was the real surprise. I'd assumed this catastrophic situation would render her a stuttering wreck, but she was calm, serene. It's a trait I'd love to say she inherits from her mother, but Aaron is the eye of the hurricane in our lives.

"You're my rock, babe," I said to him. "You know that?"

Which brought me to a bleak conundrum. He needed help. It wasn't just the blood loss or the bad leg, but the prospect of head trauma. His eyes were rolling back in his head. His blackouts were coming without warning. His speech was slurred. This man needed medical attention soon or he might die.

And the monstrously harsh reality was that to save him, I might have to leave him there.

It wasn't even midmorning yet.

CHAPTER 5

SHOULD I STAY or go find help on my own, back to that damn rock face? I was in a foreign landscape, unsure how to navigate its terrain.

But what if Aaron's skull was fractured?

I'm terrible when it comes to first aid. All I could reference in my head were flashes of random TV shows. Any instance of a chiseled ambulance driver pushing on the chest of an injured pedestrian. What did they do with the head? What did they *say* to the head?

"Sierra, I need you to do something brave for Mommy," I said to her.

She came over right away, with a generally stunned look on her face. She stood in front of me, patiently waiting for me to tell her about the next calamity.

"Sierra, I need you to press on Daddy's head."

She stood there for a moment, then said gravely, "But Daddy has a bad head."

"Yes, and that's why you have to press. Like this. See?"

I showed her. His plaid button-up shirt had enough fluff to absorb some wetness without getting soggy. I could tie it, but I didn't want to move his head any more than necessary.

I made a map in my head and did some calculations, before turning to my husband. "Aaron, honey, listen to me if you can. I'm going to leave you for about three hours. Ninety minutes out. Ninety back. That gets me five miles. Sierra will be here. I need to find help and get a helicopter for you."

I waited for a response from him. I got silence.

"Daddy wants a helicopter?" asked Sierra.

"I'm going to hike toward the junction at 89," I said to my blank husband. "That gives us the best chance of seeing traffic. Because the road we were on was pretty dead." Dead is a bad word. "I mean…I have hope…that I might see a few cars and flag one down. Maybe the SUV that hit us."

He didn't stir. Nothing.

"Aaron?" I put my hand on his shoulder.

He was still. Disturbingly still. I could barely detect any breath; he did have a pulse, but it was weak.

I took a deep breath. I turned to Sierra. I summoned my best Solemn Mom face, making sure not to enter

Scary Mom face-zone, and said, "Okay, Sierra, I need you to do something very important."

"Is Daddy sick?"

"Yes. He needs a doctor. I'm going to find one." I was ready for her to freak out that I'd be leaving. She stayed still as I continued. "The important thing is Daddy will need to rest as much as possible, so even though—"

"I can watch him," she said.

She stood there like a brave little soldier, perfectly at attention.

"You can?" I asked.

"Yeah," she nodded slowly. "I can hold Daddy Koala's paw."

"He might wake up and say strange things but don't worry, he's being silly. Just tell him that Mommy went to get a doctor, and he needs to stay still."

"Okay. Don't worry, Mommy."

"I love you, Sierra." I kissed her on the forehead and grabbed the hiking pack.

We had one granola bar left. It was murder trying to think of how to divvy this measly thing up. Some for Sierra? Some for Aaron, who probably wouldn't even eat it? Some for me, the one who might have to sprint for two hours straight? How do you divide the lone granola bars of life?

We had planned to stop for lunch in Chasm before

heading to Jed's house. Despite everything, I could hear her stomach already rumbling.

I put the whole thing in his jeans pocket and smiled at Sierra, relying on her to decide to eat it if she needed to, or sacrifice it if Daddy needed it more. Me? I was fine. I could run on pure anxiety juice. I was already overdosing on it.

I began to head out and was close to the mouth of the cave when I heard Aaron's voice behind me. He was starting to talk!

I spun around just as he was already slipping back into a deep sleep. He'd summoned every last ounce of his energy to utter a sentence that would occupy my mind for the rest of the day.

"Be careful who you trust."

CHAPTER 6

I WAS ALONE now. Not in the spiritual sense. Not in the romantic sense. But in the imperiled sense. The survival game. I was now hiking away from everything that mattered to me.

How does a small child survive in a cave? She would never leave her dad's side, but what if her dad's side left *her?* What if the unthinkable happened while I was gone? What if my husband died? What if tiny Sierra ended up there alone?

I was walking across incredibly jagged crags. Rocks sharp enough to cut flesh, rocks that could severely hurt me if I twisted my ankle. But worse than the pain if I was crippled—Sierra would be alone. No one would know where we were, where my husband was. She'd be stranded.

With that in mind, I crossed the rubble painfully slowly. The hesitation felt necessary, but it was a risk in itself; hesitation breeds bad decisions.

Be careful who you trust.

Why would Aaron tell me that, out here in the land of zero population? Nobody lives here. Nobody camps here. Nobody *was* here. I'd started to truly see it on this hike. We'd be lucky to find anyone at all.

But I had to maintain hope. *Maybe today is the day there is a nurse convention in the desert crags.* I was heading for elevation, to the closest viable ridge. From there, I figured I'd be afforded at least a twenty-mile vantage point. There was a fairly clean path up the rock face on my left that looked like a few miles of gradual slope, before zigzagging back up the hillside for another stretch of gradual slope to the top of my target ridge.

Or I could climb.

Climbing would be risky—possibly deadly—but I'd be saving myself hours of walking, a tough economization to resist. I could be up that ridge in half an hour. It wasn't steep, and limestone is a safe rock. I'd climbed tougher routes. My instincts said I could handle it.

And yet my mind kept arguing with the numbers.

This particular hill offered a decently high chance of success. Let's say 80 percent. The problem was that I'd be facing that sort of choice more than once. And every time I chose the riskier option, I'd be multiplying the risk factor times all the future risk factors. That's 80 percent times 80 percent times—

"Oh, my God, Miranda," I said out loud, "just make a decision."

I'd just wasted minutes trying to figure out how to avoid wasting minutes. So I chose to climb. I started walking toward the cliff face and was soon monkeying up it. There were handholds to grip. And the footholds I found felt solid. My confidence increased as I looked straight up and had a clear visual of most of my route.

It really didn't take long to reach the top, and I had an immediate task scheduled for myself. Research.

I'd sent up the signal flare thinking I saw sunlight glinting on a town, like maybe Red Bluff.

But I was wrong, I was now seeing a harsh reality. There was no city, no town. From this mercilessly clear vantage point I could see that what I thought was a town was . . . just a mirage. A desert mirage. The oldest cliché in the book.

I was flooded with regret. I'd sent up our only signal flare with no purpose.

With that bad news suddenly came good news—

Crack!

What sounded like a rifle shot was startlingly loud in the quiet landscape, and echoed. I didn't think it could be more than a half mile away, though I had no idea which direction.

I instantly rejoiced at the prospect of hearing hunters in the distance. My first thought was, *Humans. Salvation.* Sure, it was dangerous to have bullets flying around. Most people would rightfully cringe and take cover. But in this case, bullets were music to my ears.

Crack! The next shot echoed around me. Even closer.

I don't know what you would hunt in the desert, though.... Maybe it was a search party?

I stood tall and shouted, "Hey! Help! I need help!" I was waving my arms like crazy. "Whoever you are, please help me!"

I scanned the area, waiting for a response that didn't come.

"I'm right here!" I said even louder. "Help!"

And the valley said nothing.

"Here on this ridge!" I yelled.

I kept repeating this routine for a half minute. Until I saw something that changed my mind about how the rest of my life might unfold.

The shooter—not very far away, maybe a hundred feet at most—well, he could see me. He was looking right at me, that was clear. He was on the ridge too, on higher ground. And he was aiming at me. Directly at me. *Crack!* Another shot was fired in my direction. From him. At me.

"Hey! What the hell is wrong with you!?" I screamed.

As I recognized who he was.

Fat.

Bearded.

Ugly.

The SUV driver.

CHAPTER 7

THIS WAS AN attack. This wasn't an accident. This man was trying to shoot me.

I froze for longer than I care to admit. I always imagined that in a situation like this a thousand thoughts would race through my mind—some emotional, some practical, some an inventory of my life—but I was mentally blank. I eventually spun around and clumsily fled down the nearest slope.

I only had one viable thought in my head, not a very impressive one: to duck behind a bush.

My laughable instinct was quickly vetoed by my legs anyway, because my legs said run.

So I ran.

Movement became autonomous. I sprinted down the slope, creating a flurry of dust behind me. *Crack,* he fired another shot through the air at my back. Was this his third or fourth? Maybe his tenth, for all I knew. I'd never been shot at before. I felt irrationally insulted.

"You're shooting at me!" I yelled, turning.

Is that all I can come up with?

"Stop!" I added.

I was crouching down again, my back to the dirt slope, taking cover, trying to figure out what to do. I wasn't in charge of my voice.

The man with the gun said nothing but kept coming. He stormed across the patches of loose shale, relentlessly focused.

I knew I had to keep moving, but I couldn't see anywhere to go. I looked back and yelled again. "My name is Miranda Cooper! I'm not whoever you think I am! I don't even know you!"

If I had to identify him in a police sketch I'd say: bearded, fat, ugly. But I could add: mean, with hate in his eyes. Was this guy actually trying to ram us off the road? He seemed absolutely oblivious to what I was saying now.

Was he trying to ram my *husband* off the road?

Crack, another shot. Another miss.

Was he himself a husband? A jealous one? Did Aaron sleep with somebody? An affair?

Where *were* we headed in our minivan? To hide? In the midst of mortal peril, my crazed brain was now conjuring up all the grotesque situations that my husband could've entangled himself in. I was picturing a hotel in something like Atlanta or St. Louis. A nice one. Two hundred dollars a night. The hotel bartender announcing last call and Aaron looking at his voluptuous business partner, whoever she was, someone with a sexy neck, while they both giggled about whose room to go up to.

No.

It's not possible. Not Aaron. He was taking us on a trip to meet a new friend he'd met on the job. Some guy named Jed. My husband doesn't cheat.

And I know every wife thinks the "not him" thing, that hers is the one prince in the world who wouldn't roam; but infidelity is beneath Aaron.

The man was now close enough that I could hear his breathing and grunting over his footsteps. He was closing the gap between us, scuffling himself down the hillside across the shale.

I looked around for places to hide or for a covered path to run along. He had a rifle with a scope. I started wishing I knew enough about guns to discern if his was a hunting rifle or a cop rifle. Useless speculation.

Something else occurred to me. My first possibly non-useless idea. Go back uphill.

If he's silly enough to choose the shale-side of a hill over the limestone-side of a hill *once,* he might be silly enough to choose it a second time. A choice with consequences. Because when a rockslide happens, even if it's just a small area that collapses—you're going to go down, hard.

The trick would be to get him to chase me up the south face. I'd be unprotected if I baited him. I looked up at the potential routes, searching for safety zones. Nope. It was all exposed.

I didn't have much longer to stew on it. I just needed to gather enough confidence to traverse the steepest part of the slope. From where I was standing, it looked incredibly intimidating. *Make a decision, Miranda.* If I took a curved path, the shape of a question mark....

Crack, another a shot sailed over my crouched position. I looked down. I wasn't in the best shoes: some cross trainers I bought for the Hip Hop Cardio class I never took.

They were going to have to outperform their mission statement, though. They needed to give me traction up the only road out of hell.

CHAPTER 8

I SPRINTED UP the gravel incline just as, *crack,* another gunshot exploded in the air behind me, instantly followed by the sound of dirt puffing up by my feet. He was getting closer. I kept climbing. This was only going to work if I managed to do one particular thing—not get hit by a bullet.

I hadn't realized how insane my plan was until I was fully exposed on the rock face. I'm sure I looked like the biggest target this whacko had ever seen. Yet there I was, heading up the cliff as fast as I could, in the strategic path of a question mark.

He started running up behind me. He really did. Straight upward, the cheat. And I began to believe this entire ploy might just work.

If he would enter the slide zone, I'd gain about five minutes on him. The rocks would tangle him up. He might sprain an ankle. At the *very* least, he'd slide all the way back down and be bewildered. I'd be free to make a mad dash. I might even manage to separate him from his gun.

Crack—another shot. Missed, but splattered the dust directly near my hand.

I could see him fiddle with the gun. Because it was broken?—no, to reload it. He was coming up a lot faster than I anticipated. I was just nearing the top and he was already nearing the end of the loose shale, a patch of hillside about the size of a grocery store aisle. He'd already traversed most of it fast, surprisingly without incident. What was motivating this idiot?

The footing beneath him was holding up agonizingly well, and I'd stopped to *watch* all this, letting him gain on me, assuming I'd have already achieved the desired landslide by now. No such luck.

I'm not sure what I did to give him road rage but now he'd taken it off the road. Was life so bad in the wild west that people chased after fellow motorists on foot?

"I'm just a mother!" I yelled at him.

He was nearly across the band of "helpful" geology. I was nearly at the end of my safety zone. The rest of my climb was going to put me in a long corridor of easiest targeting. *Crack,* he fired another shot at me.

And then his foot plunged.

Downward. Deep. I didn't see it at first but I heard it. I'd ducked down after the last bullet whizzed by my head (note, Miranda, the best time to duck is *before* the deadly projectile arrives, not after), but I heard something like miniature thunder down below me. I heard, yes, a rock slide. It was like thunder, or a bowling alley.

I looked down, and not only was he sliding down the slope, as I'd hoped, but the entire diagonal section of rocks cascaded with him. He was riding a magic carpet of sharp, jagged stones. The avalanche knocked him off his feet—the point a guardian angel should step in—and, dumbfounded, I watched him plummet all the way down to the hard ground of the ravine. *Didn't see that coming.*

The only sign of the disturbance was an elongated cloud of dust rising below. But he was down there. In bad shape. He had to have fallen a hundred feet.

I strained to see through the dust and detected a crumpled heap of errantly strewn limbs, lying motionless. His leg was rotated awkwardly outward, probably broken.

Okay, what now? The only route down was to march back down past him. But what if he was faking it? What if he was waiting until I got close, to shoot me, up close and personal?

I picked up the sharpest piece of shale I could find. It felt heavy enough to do damage, but light enough to throw. Maybe I could spin it at him like a Frisbee.

I started scooting down the hillside, trying and failing to be quiet. He hadn't yet looked up or moved. *Spinning a rock like a Frisbee is ridiculous. What is wrong with you, Miranda?* I could see him more clearly as I got closer. He was sprawled, facedown. It felt very likely that I would tumble forward to plummet as he had, and land right on top of him, dead.

I held my rock-weapon up, like a quarterback ready to throw.

"You almost killed my daughter!" I shouted.

I wanted to just throw my projectile at him, but I had some more choice words. "My daughter...she's four! And you were shooting at me! Why?!"

He really was quite still. I knew I should walk away, continue on to get help for Aaron—every moment counted. But I felt drawn to see him up close—to know what we were dealing with.

"Hey!" I said. "Hey, I'm right here with a sharp rock! You don't have to pretend to be out! You don't have to fake it."

I started to wonder if he was still breathing. I moved between him and his rifle, lying in the dirt about ten feet away. I kept my shale-football-Frisbee-rock-spear held high above me, and felt the clichés bubbling to my mouth.

"One false move, buster, and you're going down in flames!"

Flames? I knelt by his side. I needed to flip him over. *Buster?*

I steeled myself. He might lunge at me. He might turn out to be someone I knew. He might be someone whose identity made sense and somehow proved to me that Aaron wasn't a good husband. Every part of my brain started whirling. I pushed at his shoulder and stomach and managed to flip him over.

It was horrible. His face was torn open.

"Are you okay?" I asked in a nice, maternal tone of voice. "Can you breathe?"

This man was certainly no friend of mine. But faced with a dying human, I couldn't just walk away. I had to do something.

There are so many times I've told myself I need to take CPR. So many times Aaron and I decided that to be good parents, we had to be experts in resuscitation. Who knew when we might need to revive Sierra? Or each other? Or our dog? I had read the steps—but here I was, feeling helpless. I knew there was pressing, and counting....

"Hey, man, wake up!"

In the heat of the moment, I was panicking. I was increasing my anxiety by the minute. *I killed this man.* I put my hands on his chest. To press.

Step one. Ask, "Hey, are you okay?"

Step two. Check for breathing and pulse. Not breathing. But he had a pulse, though it was weak.

Step three. Chest compressions. I vaguely remembered some trick with the song "Another One Bites the Dust," which sets the cadence for the chest compressions. Ironic, given the circumstances. Did he even need chest compressions? *I killed him. It was my plan to trip him down the mountain.*

Step four. Call for help.

If I yelled out for help, out here approximately one billion miles from the nearest anything, no one would come. But if I were to *call. . . .*

That's when the obvious dawned on me. I didn't have a phone, but he did. He must. More important than his gun, I could take his phone.

Save him first, Miranda.

I would revive him, then find the phone, call 911, and request an ambulance for him and helicopter for my husband. The new plan. I leaned over to start the compressions.

But before I could even touch his chest, he coughed.

He was awake.

"Hey!" I yelled. "Hey, you're up! You're okay? Are you? Can you breathe?"

No words came out, just a terrible sound.

"My name is Miranda. You just fell down a mountain."

He coughed and up came blood. Lots of blood. It was in his lungs. Whatever the problem was, he had ruptured something vital, deep within him. He burbled up a crimson stream that trickled down his chin and cheeks.

"Tellth..." he said to me.

"What?"

"Tell..." he said. He stopped. Then he continued. "Them."

"Them? Who? Okay, I will. Tell what?"

It took a moment, but he finally answered. "My team...to save me."

"What team?"

Team? Did he say team?

"Was there someone else in the car with you?" I asked. "Did you ram me off the road?"

I needed to give this man time to respond.

"Why did your team ram me off the road?"

He was dying. Now. Here.

"T-tray..." he said weakly. Was this his dying breath? He looked over at me.

"No," I said. I would not let him quit. "No way. Stay awake, buddy. Please."

"Kiss," he said.

"Don't give up, man!" How had I gone from a road trip with my family to watching a man I didn't know die?

"Tray," he gasped, then started again. "Tray…Kiss… Kilt…" and then a big exhale…

And he was gone.

CHAPTER 9

HE DIED. RIGHT there in front of me. I watched a human being leave this world. At thirty years of age, I was lucky—this was the first time I'd ever seen someone go.

I stood up, feeling heavy and sick to my stomach. My head was swirling. My face was sweating cold droplets down my brow. Before I knew what was happening, I gave way to my nausea, sending my upper body folding forward with hands braced against my thighs. *I did this to him.* I sent him up the loose shale. I ended a man's life. No matter what kind of idiotic warfare he had waged on me, I'm not in the business of ending lives. And I'd just ended one.

"Damn it, Mandy."

I took a few breaths, got my bearings, and knelt by him again.

I began a prayer. A silent one, not words but more feelings. Putting aside the guilt that threatened to overwhelm me, I prayed for him to be forgiven, to see a better place than whatever chaotic evil had led him to a life of chasing innocent women through the desert with a rifle.

Or was he chasing Aaron?

"Tray. Kiss. Kilt," I said to myself. What in God's name could that mean?

I unpressed my palms and stood back up.

I had to be careful. This man mentioned others. The rest of his "team," so I could assume that there were other fine gentlemen in the car that ran us off the road. If he was now in my canyon, shooting at me, what were these "others" doing?

I drew a little map on the dirt with a stick. The river. The highway. The cliff we tumbled over. The spot where our van was sprawled out like a turtle on its back. The waterfall. The crags. The cave containing my husband and child.

As far as I could tell, this guy, this corpse next to me, got lucky finding me out here on the south end of the canyon. Unless he had tracked me in a more sophisticated way than I was aware of, he wasn't expecting me to be right here. The safer place to look—where I was betting his team was right now—was the area very close to the highway where we were run off.

So my new goal was to get to the main highway we were headed toward. A big eight-lane behemoth of glory.

Tray. Kiss. Kilt. I picked up Mr. SUV Driver's rifle. It was scratched but didn't look broken. I tried to cock it, but the gun didn't cooperate.

Then I remembered—*the phone!*

I quickly turned back to him. I'd completely forgotten. I dug for his phone in his pocket, found it, and tried to turn it on. It was locked, as expected, but I should at least be able to dial 911, which I did…but got nothing. We were so far away from any signal, even a priority call wouldn't get through.

I put it in my pocket, to try again later.

Tray. Kiss. Kilt.

I stood up and erased my map in the dirt with my shoe.

Kiss. Maybe I'd been onto something before, and Aaron really had kissed this guy's wife. That made sense. No. No, it didn't.

Why would Mr. SUV Driver bring all his friends? His driving maneuver seemed too premeditated for a crime of passion.

Who exactly was this "Jed" we were visiting? He supposedly had a ranch and lovely horses, fine, but why suddenly visit a guy we barely knew? Why had I agreed to this visit I knew nothing about?

Maybe he kissed some girl at work? But no, I didn't think there were many single mingling types at Drake Oil.

I noticed my shadow on the ground. There was my

silhouette, unchanged but for the gun in hand. I was that woman. The gun woman.

My shadow seemed to belong to a different person.

Armed with a gun, a phone, and a new sense of purpose, I hiked over to the crest of the ridge. *Tray Kiss.* Maybe it's actually *Drake Is*. I was replaying the audio in my head, not just the words. I was scrutinizing the nuances. Tray Kiss. *Drake Is.* The dead SUV driver was saying *Drake Is* Something.

"Drake is…" I said to myself, imitating his voice.

The more I thought about it, the more I couldn't imagine any other possibility.

What I was hoping to achieve was a good view of the back canyon. This was about a two-mile corridor. If Mr. SUV Driver had hiked through here, maybe his teammates were nearby. Fine. As bad as it sounded, I preferred this possibility to its catastrophic alternative: enemies might be heading toward my *family,* toward my injured husband and my tiny daughter. If they were willing to shoot at me—I mean, no questions asked, just shoot at me—what would they do to my daughter?

No way, not letting that happen. I needed to survey the terrain as fast as possible and plot a countermeasure. I sped up to a run, now among the top crags.

Drake. Is. Kilt. This was about my husband. This was

about something he did. Said. I was replaying every aspect of Mr. SUV Driver's voice in my head. *Drake. Is. Kilt. Exhale.* And I was now starting to hear the end of his speech a little differently. There was more of a word tucked in there. Drake. Is. Kilt. Something.

I was on the crest now, viewing the expanse of the valley. I could see the arroyo where Mr. SUV Driver first greeted me with his bullets.

Drake is *guilty.*

I finally heard it for what it was. Guilty. *Drake,* the oil company, *is guilty.*

But I couldn't let the mental gyrations distract me from the puzzle in front of me. If there were other men out there, and Mr. SUV Driver came from the top of the far crest…they probably split up right before the crest. There—tracing his trail upward with my eyes I could see the other path, the one they might have followed. It led back to the crags. And that meant that they were already on their way back to Aaron and Sierra.

Unacceptable. I needed them to go anywhere but into my nest.

Panic set in, flooding me with nervous, hand-wringing energy. But I already knew what I had to do.

There was no more time to waste.

I raised the rifle upward. I committed myself to a plan that would spur this cat-and-mouse game to its inevitable conclusion. I held it with both hands. Straight upward. Like I've seen on TV.

I fired, once. *Bam.* The recoil nearly knocked me to the ground, and the sound was startling, tearing into the soft silence.

You hear that, gentlemen? Bring it.

CHAPTER 10

DRAKE OIL IS a fine, fine oil institution. A group of nice people who just want to help America and kittens.

That's what the ads would have you believe.

And that's what the press would have you believe. The articles. The billboards. The way the cute logo was cutely designed. And, most of all, the way the quiet legal disagreements were quietly settled. Thanks to my husband.

This I knew. He is, after all, one of their lawyers.

I was running as fast I could. Sure, I was trying to get them to follow me; but I couldn't let them actually *get* me. I was going as fast as I could for as long as I could.

Without wind, this was the quietest space you can imagine. It was so still you could actually hear the silence. This was helpful. I should be able to hear anyone coming from behind me. When I stopped, every so often, I could listen.

There was nothing.

"Keep moving," I whispered to myself.

My mind raced. Jesus, did my husband piss off somebody who settled a suit with Drake Oil? Who then needed vengeance on my family?

I continued this way, running as fast as my burning legs would allow, for what seemed like an hour. There were no footstep sounds behind me yet, but plodding along like the opposite of a ninja, I suddenly, faintly, heard someone yell something in the distance.

I stopped, trying to muffle my own panting. I needed to examine the silence, searching the air for the distinct sound of what I thought was a man's shout.

Heart slamming against my breastbone, even my pulse became deafening.

I scanned the horizon behind me, the outline of the red columns of rock, searching for traces of a human shape. Probably one aiming a gun at me.

What in the world did Aaron do to get people to *coordinate* an attack against him? Did he stumble into something dangerous? The silence and stillness held no answers.

I got moving again. My legs were cramping, the stopping and starting becoming harder for my body to execute.

Aaron hadn't said anything to me, but I imagined that his daily access to the entire legal landscape of Drake must have given him a glimpse of something insidious. He would've kept it secret from me, for fear that my unstoppable lungs would have bellowed it to anyone who'd listen. I couldn't blame him. He was right.

I worked my way back up to a full sprint, capitalizing on the downhill grade, ignoring the cramps and the strains. I was nearing a huge area of boulders nestled near the river, coming around a blind corner, top speed, when the following disaster happened faster than I could process:

1. I heard a pop.
2. I crashed into an obstacle I didn't think would be there and bounced off.
3. I realized it was a man.
4. He and I locked eyes in a moment of mutual shock.
5. We agreed not to be friends.

CHAPTER 11

HE WAS A mercenary. In what felt like one millisecond after our collision, he decked me across the jaw, *hard.* I recoiled backward. If Mr. SUV Driver was a dangerous man, this second guy was a nuclear war.

You could see it in his eyes: this wasn't a person, this was a professional killer. He was dressed for attacking things—soldier pants, Kevlar vest, handgun, hiking boots.

I was on my back. I'd never been hit before. Not even my older sister, Valentina, would punch me. We were slappers and that ended at age nine.

I had surprised him, but well-trained instinct enabled him to regain the upper hand. I would've assumed, prior to this moment of my life, that it would hurt to get hit; but it actually was too shocking. I hadn't read the "So You're About to Be Punched in the Jaw" orientation brochure, but it might explain that with the hit, your grasp on reality vaporizes. You get stupider.

So there I was, on the dirt, catching up with my current reality. He was slowly approaching me but I was too cloudy to even scoot myself backward. I just stayed there. Done.

And then my enemy noticed something, at the same moment that I did.

He stopped in his tracks, a bewildered expression now on his face, replacing the steel of a moment before. He was looking down at his left hand, palm-up as if checking for raindrops. The raindrop was red, and it had come from his shoulder.

He had been shot. By me.

CHAPTER 12

I VAGUELY REMEMBERED hearing a pop. That was the sound of my gun going off, though I hadn't realized it way back seven seconds ago. I'd been carrying my rifle, running along rather blithely with my hand loosely on the trigger, when I slammed into the back of him. A car rear-ending another car. Thrown to the ground when he punched me, I must've pulled the trigger.

The whole transaction had taken place in the blink of an eye. The bullet must have entered him in the shoulder and exited in the upper part of his back. I'd been quite certain I'd walked into my own execution just now. Yet here we were, both motionless, both in shock.

He began to inspect himself beyond his palm, noting the expanding circle of blood on his shirt. His injury looked severe.

But not crippling.

"Now" flashed in my mind. I scrambled for the gun (who is this new Miranda, operating my body?), which

had fallen to my side. I fumbled, grabbed it, and spun to take aim. He dove forward, right at me. I got lucky once, but rifles are not effective close-range weapons, which he proved by diving on me.

Our fight wasn't over. Our fight had just begun.

Thank God there was a bullet in him, or through him, because this was the strongest living organism I had ever put my hands on. I used to playfight with Aaron in bed, knew his contours and weaknesses. These muscles here, from Mr. Kevlar, were unbelievable. Hard as rock. Huge. And trying to kill me.

I desperately curled into a fetal position and received a hit in the ribs that took my breath away. *Oh, God.* I caught his wrist and clung to it, in a weak attempt to disable one of those bionic arms. This would be painfully fast—I'd be knocked out with two more punches. But I dimly realized we had begun rolling.

Toward the river.

He pulled me into him, trying to bring my head down to knee my face like it was a martial arts fight on TV, but I used all my strength to turn away from his right side. I was, in effect, cranking the two of us in a sideways tango downhill, toward the river.

We rolled at first slowly, quarter turn by quarter turn, as he battered me with his fist. Before, I'd been too shocked for his hits to register. Well, now, I was exquisitely feeling them. Every single one. The head, the neck, the head again, the ribs, trying to get me to release my grip.

My grip?

I somehow had my hands gripped around his throat now.

My fingers clutched as hard as they could, a relentless hold on his nape, with my thumbs pushing into his voice box. My own strength surprised me. Call it rage, call it maternal instinct, call it whatever you want—I was operating under the influence of pure adrenaline. I was much smaller than this man, but he was now up against a climber's hands. My grip was life or death.

"Who are you?" I said through gritted teeth. Our faces were close enough that I could see the vessels around his pupils.

Then the horizon began to flip over behind him. We were rolling. But I didn't care. I was peering deep into his eyes.

"Who are you?!" I repeated as the horizon continued to turn, as we tumbled toward the last ledge on the cliff.

He didn't blink, even more of an automaton than Mr. SUV Driver.

He hit me again. I withstood it. I don't know how. Simply adrenaline? I knew that my gun was on the ground, back up where we started rolling. If he would just be so kind as to cooperate by letting go of me, I could go get it and shoot him again.

"Are you Drake?" I asked him, grunting as we grappled. I asked again, "Are you Drake Oil?"

It felt like I'd been on the ground with this man for a full year of my life, yet there I was—still alive, still a contender. In my favor was the fact that his bullet wound wasn't just one hole, it was two. I knew because I was covered in his blood from rolling in the dirt. I was beginning to see I had hope.

Until we splashed in the river.

I didn't register being midair, but I definitely noticed when the free fall finished and we plunged into turbulent, cascading water. My world went cold as we were dunked under and instantly swept along.

His grip softened just a bit; it was all I'd hoped for in these interminable minutes. Let that be printed on my tombstone: SHE GOT HIM TO SOFTEN HIS GRIP.

But he was on top still, his formidable body weight shoving me deeper down. We banged limbs for what seemed like the entire month of June. I suppose I should've been worried about upcoming rocks, but he'd introduced a new variable into the equation—not sure when that was exactly. He had a knife.

Underwater, amid murky eddies, I didn't have his throat anymore. I had both of my hands on his wrist.

My instincts had rerouted all my physical focus from his esophagus to the jagged, murderous blade in his fist.

One swipe, one cut, and I would've been done.

With rocks on all sides, we were getting up close and personal with the unforgiving wrecking balls of the rapids. My one goal was to try to swim upward, break free of his iron grip, and get to the surface. I could engage instead, try some kung fu moves on his face—but I'm not the fastest thinker when it comes to underwater close-quarters death-match combat.

Didn't matter. The game ended on its own.

His size was his advantage on land, but it became his Achilles' heel in the rapids. He was too big to make it safely through the rocks unscathed. The riverbed did its job.

Poonk. A muffled thud. I could hear the blow his head took from a cluster of granite. He swung his last two punches at me in a half-hearted, half-conscious motion.

His grip on me faded.

The surface seemed to rush down toward my face, and my body emerged like a clumsy rocket. I had been treading so hard, I actually got my full torso up above the waterline before being beaten back down by the current. I was floating. I tried to glance behind me to see if he'd surface, too. We'd both been under what felt like a decade. I scanned the surface behind me but he'd been consumed. I assumed, given the gunshot and blood loss, that he was dead.

And I was adrift.

I slowly took inventory of the situation: where I was heading, where I'd been, and what I now had in my possession.

I had nothing. The river gave me victory but it stripped me of all else. In addition to the gun I'd already lost, I'd lost my jacket. I'd lost my phone. The only thing I didn't lose was pants, and a clear sense that things were going to get worse before they got better.

CHAPTER 13

I MANAGED TO drift over to the riverbank and crawl up onto dry land, dragging my torso above the waterline. It was a Herculean effort, though pathetic. To an onlooker, I'd appear to be a major drama queen. One hand slowly clawing after another. Pulling in slow motion. Gasping.

I'd kill to see anyone out here...of course, I've killed the two people I've run into so far.

But I was alone, having led myself a million miles away from hope. All I had were wet clothes and unanswered questions. Why Drake Oil? Why my husband? Where's a phone?

I needed physically proficient help. I needed a cop. Better yet, an FBI task force.

Where to go now? The crags were south. The freeway north.

My husband, in the crags, might need me. I could give him an update on my trials out here in the wild.

And he could tell me whatever he might have to tell me. Like, y'know: *Miranda, funny thing I should've mentioned; here's why an army of men might try to kill you on your stroll through the western United States.*

The possibility of actual help, though, was north. A busy highway. The bigger highway gave me the best chance of finding a good Samaritan, and then law enforcement.

Yet what would I even say? Even if I managed to flag down a speeding motorist by the side of a highway at night, what if he or she didn't believe me? Even if I managed to find the nearest police force, how would that story go?

"Officer, I need your help," I said aloud, rehearsing. "I...uh...I..." Talking things out always helps me when I'm overwhelmed; it comes naturally to me. And right now, exhausted, starving, battered, half drowned, I felt half insane. Why not make an imaginary friend while I was at it? Anything to keep me going.

I took a few gradual steps along the higher slope. I would, again, hike to the nearest vista point, so I could make an informed decision.

"Excuse me, officer," I repeated to the imaginary cop.

"What seems to be the trouble, miss?" I said back to myself. Slight southern accent.

"Well...you see...Drake Oil."

"Reckon I don't follow," I said, tilting up my imaginary cowboy hat. I decided I had on boots and spurs. A female deputy detective.

"For a bite of your éclair," I said to her, "I'll tell you."

I took a bite out of the phantom detective's phantom éclair. And noted that my hunger level was starting to get to me.

"He started working for Drake Oil three years ago," I said.

"Who?" said the detective.

"My husband."

"I thought you said you were the one in oil."

"We both—"

"Skip the foo foo," said the detective. "Tell me facts. Just the facts. Three sentences. Go."

I was already a mile through the canyon, by my reckoning. The clock was spinning unforgivingly in my head. My imaginary detective had no patience. So I got to the point.

"Once upon a time this really awesome chick with a sharp wit and tendency to say exactly what she thinks met a man named Aaron Cooper, who made her heart glow. Like E.T.'s finger would glow. We both had… *have*…a love of the great outdoors. I was doing geological survey work for oil drilling and he was doing legal work out in the field. We had noble aspirations to help make the world a better…"

"Ma'am."

"Sorry. The point is that soon I became a full-time mom. And my husband got promoted at Drake Oil. And I never thought I'd be up against murderers." I started to lose my train of thought. "What could my husband mean about trust?"

"What?" said the detective.

"Trust. Who I'd trust. What did he mean?"

More important than answers is keeping my family safe. The only assurance of that was to keep the wolves as far away from the front yard as possible.

"You can trust whoever earns it," said the detective.

As badly as I wanted to go back to Sierra and Aaron, interrogate him about what he'd meant by his cryptic warnings, I decided to steer my enemies in the other direction. If I'd identified the voices correctly, there had to be at least one left. And if he, or they, were following me, tracking me, listening to me, then I was now devoted to keeping them up north.

I turned immediately to march in that direction. I didn't walk to stay hidden. I walked to move fast. *Find the highway. Find the cop.* I guessed that it would be three miles, but took shortcuts wherever the topography would allow it. Cutting across the rock face. Occasionally jogging. And with that determination I wound up all the way on the north rim of the canyon.

Daylight was waning. Ugly things were happening all around me and I was pretending I was fine with that. I was pretending I could chitchat with imaginary cops and that I hadn't killed two people. Most of all, I was pretending I wasn't terrified out of my mind. The truth was if I let reality hit me, I would crumple.

So I had to lie to myself, had to think that I could make things work out. When darkness had undeniably fallen, I found some scrub that I could sleep in that would hide me well enough. It wouldn't hide me from the cold, but I was less worried about the cold than the bullets. I was worried about Aaron and Sierra, of course, but I had to assume they were safe in the cave. I didn't think there was any way that I would sleep—but the events of the day had taken its toll, and I was soon dreaming of food and water and big koala hugs.

CHAPTER 14

AFTER SOME AMOUNT of time I awoke. Maybe it had all been a dream! But no, here I was in a maze of tall, slender rock formations, short coffee-less minutes after waking. It was dangerous to be up here, a treacherous jungle gym of limestone, but it was worth it. I'd found a vantage point to finally behold: the Grail.

Up ahead in the distance was Highway 89, strewn gloriously across the desert like an umbilical cord to salvation.

I'd never been so happy to see concrete. Cars zipped by in the distance—happy families on their happy ways. It was a giddy feeling of hope I hadn't experienced in quite some time. It was intoxicating, mental bliss. And it was precisely what got me in trouble.

There were voices around me. Men. Nearby. I hadn't noticed until it was too late. Two men. Getting louder. Getting closer. Even from my vantage point, I couldn't see where they were but I could hear one shouting directions to the other. And I soon caught his name.

"Clay! Down this way?"

"No, go uphill from where you are," shouted Clay. "Can't you see the one stack that's in shadow?"

Clay was the man in charge. They must've gotten lost, or separated.

"Where?" shouted the guy who wasn't Clay. "I can't see it."

They were practically on top of me. There'd be no turning around without getting caught. Thankfully, they couldn't see each other or me, although I did manage to catch a glimpse of Clay. He was clean-cut, corporate, athletic, matching the smart rasp in his voice. Seemingly not a mercenary like the first two I'd met...but still paralyzed me with fear.

They had guns. And I didn't.

But they didn't *know* I didn't.

I had an opportunity, albeit a scary one. I took a deep breath. I needed my voice to reverberate throughout the cathedral of rocks and throughout their souls. I would need those men to tremble. I would need them to believe I was pointing a rifle at them.

So I cleared my throat, steeled my voice, and bellowed my opening gambit. *"Move and I'll kill you."*

CHAPTER 15

THEY BOTH STOPPED talking. After an eternity I heard some quick, quiet scrambling. Then total silence.

My heart was pounding so loud I was sure they would echo-locate me by its beat. I couldn't see Clay, but I knew he was across the rock colony, about thirty feet away from me. Eventually I could hear him again. He was quietly guiding his partner around the maze with shrill whispers.

All three of us were now blindly situated in a deadly game of Marco Polo.

I kept track of their chatter and managed to intercept some of his hushed commands, thereby piecing together my own plan of attack: how to move, where to move, when to move. I had the upper hand. From my hidden perch, I would give them enough phony clues to convince them I was watching them the whole time. Then, with clever wording, I could get them to put their guns on the ground and back away.

Brilliant, right?

Wrong.

Suddenly, I looked around to realize that *I* was the one being gamed. Clay was baiting *me,* knowing that I could hear his last round of whispering. He was just loud enough that I could catch his details, not loud enough that it was obvious.

He'd lured me to crawl into what I now saw was a central cluster of the rock formation. He'd orchestrated our rendezvous.

I was in serious trouble.

I expected him to get quiet now that he had me where he wanted, but he talked directly to me.

"Miranda," he said. Not shouting but projecting. Like a Greek orator. Saying my name like a dad would say it, like he was addressing his teenage kid who was caught sneaking back into the house at two a.m.

"Miranda," he repeated.

I didn't answer.

"My name is Clay Hobson."

He couldn't see me. Though he ensnared me, he still didn't know exactly where I was or whether I was armed. It was a miracle he and his pet thug hadn't stormed my nook. If they did, both of them at once, I'd be cornered in broad daylight. It'd be over.

But they weren't coming.

"I'm not here to hurt you," said Clay.

Yeah, right, you can fertilize the lawn with that one.

"I'm not here to hurt your family, Miranda."

He was playing verbal chess.

"I'm here to help," he added. "We both are."

I was too scared to retort but I couldn't afford to stay quiet. I needed to assert some kind of competitive quality. My silence was a giant white flag, being waved like a sheet of Kleenex, indicating I was weak.

"I'm Clay and my partner's name is Terrence Unger. We're worried about your husband."

"You can fertilize the lawn!" I yelled.

He went quiet. The lawn? That was *not* what I wanted to say. That was the worst phrase possible. I strained to listen for them trading more instructions, but I could only hear the nearby rapids, which certainly didn't help. Every splash and babble seemed to have Clay's communications hidden within it.

"Miranda." He finally spoke up again. "I'm sorry about the other two gentlemen you met. They were hostile to you. And that's inexcusable. The truth is—"

"If you touch my daughter, I'll kill you!" I shouted.

"Not everyone in our little group is agreeing on how to proceed," he finished. "Yes, absolutely, if I touch your daughter, please kill me. I'm not here to do anything but help you and help your daughter. And especially help Aaron. Where is Aaron?"

Directly north.

That's what I wanted to say—the opposite of where he really was. But I knew this statement would be too elementary. Clay would have to assume I'm suggesting the opposite direction. He would go south. And he would find my family.

"Miranda?" shouted Clay.

Then he stopped talking. The other guy—his partner, or goon, or rent-a-thug—was quietly asking about something that almost sounded like the word *dynamite.*

"Wish we had some of that dynamite here," he murmured.

Dynamite?

"It's at the ranch," Clay murmured back. "With Branch. Wish we could use it on that strike."

Dynamite for what? And what's the branch he mentioned? What kind of strike were they planning?

"Miranda, do you need food?" said Clay loudly.

I didn't have a wristwatch but I could tell our standoff had been going on for a while.

"We have food," he added. "Do you need some?"

The stalemate was seductive. Simply the opportunity to eat something felt irresistible. Yet as we kept talking in circles, I was beginning to realize Clay's game was deadlier than I thought. It was only after the third round of silence that I pinpointed it but I could hear him mumbling very quietly again, which I'd assumed was to his partner, but he wasn't talking to him.

Clay was on the phone. Clay had *been* on the phone.

"Where is Aaron?" he randomly said aloud to me again, this time in an even nicer tone than before. Then he resumed murmuring.

A phone call. He must have been using a satellite phone, like we used when doing survey work in remote locations.

Clay wasn't playing mind games to get me to move, he was manipulating me to keep me still.

CHAPTER 16

I PROBABLY SHOULD'VE been more strategic. I could have waited a moment and at least calculated some defensive geometry. But I jumped up and left, with no plan or preparation. I jumped up and sprinted.

My new friend Clay Hobson had been summoning his extra troops. He'd pinned me down and held me at bay while he gathered his forces. I cursed myself for being so gullible.

But now I was sprinting full speed in the opposite direction. Away from the highway.

The game had changed. The call had changed everything. I had to get to Aaron and Sierra.

Call it willpower. Call it fear. Call it ovaries. The point is I ran so hard that I stopped caring about things like pain and air. My leg muscles were scalding, my lungs were screaming, but I didn't care. I ignored it.

I came stumbling up the crags, stumbling toward the cave entrance, and nearly collapsed. Only now did

I notice that my leg was bleeding. So was my mouth, actually. I'd dry-heaved so hard—gasping for breath, failing to swallow, failing to dampen the palate—that I scorched the back of my throat. I spat blood. I was far from caring.

I was 100 percent preoccupied with the cave I'd finally reached, worried—no, terrified—that I'd be walking into a tomb. They'd spent a night in here and I was ready to find a mortified child huddled over a stiff corpse with a single, diagonal beam of sunlight cracking through the darkness from above, illuminating them like a medieval painting.

And that's exactly what I saw. Minus the sunbeam. Minus the corpse.

"Mommy!" said Sierra from the far corner of the darkness. She jumped up, dissolving into tears.

We embraced for what must've been a three-week hug. She clamped onto my chest and I looked across the cave to find Aaron looking back at me. He'd been asleep until Sierra's joy had roused him, energized him. I can only imagine the fear they'd felt since I'd left.

As I gathered Sierra in my arms and approached my husband, I could see that his cheerful disposition was a facade. He was in bad shape. His skin was ghostly pale and there was a hollow quality to his eyes. I'd been the one fistfighting all day, but it seemed like he took every one of the blows. He looked a decade older than he did yesterday. The happy man who was in the backseat of the minivan with my daughter, navigating the kangaroo galaxy, was barely in the same cave with us now. He was a stranger.

"M…randa," he said.

The whole run back I'd been tallying up a million questions for him that, under normal circumstances, I would've launched into with guns blazing. As if anything about any of this was normal.

"I'm here for you," I said to him. No questions. Just love.

"You found…?" he struggled to speak. "You found them?"

It took a moment for me to understand what he meant.

"Yes," I replied.

"They tried…"

"To kill me? Yes."

"Then we ha…Then we have some…talking…to do." Every syllable a struggle.

"No."

"Cases…"

"Not now, babe."

"I can…explain." He gathered himself. "Drake. I saw…I've been trying…to find a way to…"

"Aaron, not now." I had to interrupt this. I couldn't let him drain his precious resources. "Listen. If you love me..." Yes, I was pulling the *if you love me* card. "If you love me...then you'll do what I'm about to tell you. No questions asked."

He answered without hesitation. "Anything."

My true ally.

"You want me to wear leather chaps?" said Aaron. "And a cowboy hat?"

"No," I replied.

"I'll do it. If that's your thing."

Oh, suddenly now he has perfect speech?

"My thing is brains," I said. "You know that."

"Brains and a leather hat." He was trying to crack a smile.

Men.

Sierra hadn't left my arms since I'd returned.

"Sierra, help me lift Daddy's legs," I said as I shot Aaron a single-upturned-eyebrow glare. "You know our very impressionable four-year-old daughter is listening."

It was reassuring to know that even in the worst of circumstances, we were still the biggest flirts of all time.

"Save your strength," I whispered.

"Don't yell at a dying man," he said, his smile just shy of a grimace.

"You are *not* dying."

We all went still. I'd raised my voice for the first time perhaps in years. Before I could go on, he mustered all his strength and spoke clearly.

"I know this doesn't make any sense. And these guys are…no joke. But I trust that you…can protect Sierra."

I didn't want him to keep going.

But he had more. "You're smarter than them, Miranda. You're the smartest person I know."

I hate compliments like that, praise from blind faith. I hate them and love them.

He added, "You just tend to doubt yourself."

"Yeah," said Sierra.

"Now," said Aaron, shifting gears. "What is this horrible thing you're about to ask me to do? Eat broccoli?"

I took a deep breath and looked over at our daughter. She had her hair in a loose, half-finished side-braid. She learned it on the internet last month. This would not be easy for them. It wasn't even easy for me to think.

"I need you to climb," I said. "I need you to climb."

CHAPTER 17

THEY WERE COMING, I explained to Aaron and Sierra. The bad men were preparing to converge on our little sanctuary. The cave was no longer safe.

I knew it was now or never.

"Okay. We can do this," said Aaron.

"Me, too," said Sierra.

Within minutes I'd gathered up my two ambassadors to begin the hobble. We each drank from the canteen. Getting Aaron to his feet was more about courage than muscle. He seemed about ten terrifying pounds lighter than when I last saw him. He barely stood upright, even with my support. Sierra could topple him just by tugging on his sleeve.

"We have only one shot at this," I began my speech. "We have to get their car."

He didn't respond.

I continued. "Clay Hobson. We have to get the SUV he was in. I'm guessing they parked somewhere on the stretch of road above our wreck. If it's still there, it's our one chance."

I glanced at his face. I had already composed the rebuttal to his upcoming rebuttal.

"Believe me, I looked," I said. "I looked for a random car, for a cop, a hiker, pay phone, a wad of promising trash. Anything. Any hope. I tried the roads. I tried to get to 89, but Clay blocked the way."

Aaron's face was unmoved. I don't know if it was stoicism or loss of blood, but his reaction was as calm as could be expected.

"You've gotta get to the SUV. If you follow the river upstream past where we crashed, there's a steep grade leading up to where we went off the highway. It's going to be a tough climb, but it's our only chance."

"If my wife wants me to climb..." he said with a smile, "then, ladies and gentlemen, I'm climbing."

Sierra was walking alongside us. She would normally get carried by him across terrain like this. But Aaron wouldn't have enough strength. So I crouched down to be eye level with my new lieutenant.

"Hey little koala, how are you and your cute paws?"

"Okay," said Sierra.

"Thank you for being a good nurse. Now I'm going to promote you to Minister of Security and Transportation. Can you handle that job?"

"Okay."

I looked up at Aaron and smiled at him.

His voice was undeniably grim. "You're not coming with us, are you?" I could hear him trying to hide his concern.

I felt so sorry for them.

"I've mulled it over a thousand ways," I replied. "This is the only one that has a chance."

"Your Transport Minister doesn't approve," he joked. Half joking.

Sierra looked up at him and then over at me. She's the world's feistiest four-year-old, but you'd never guess it here. She seemed to sense the intensity of the situation even through our veiled updates.

I kissed her and stood up. As much as I hated to part ways, I turned around and started my journey.

"Wait," said Aaron. "Why head to the SUV if we can't even unlock the door?"

I knew my answer would lead to more questions and none of us had the time, nor the blood sugar for it, so I replied without turning back. "Because I'm gonna go get the keys."

CHAPTER 18

THEY WENT ONE way. I went the other. If you drew it in the dirt, you'd have a diagram that looked like a badly written V. Actually, a curvy V. Like a bird, sort of.

I didn't want to turn around to look. I was denying finality, and looking back meant capturing a mental image that I couldn't afford to fixate on.

But several minutes later I couldn't stop myself.

They were a half mile away from me, my poor, slow-moving duo.

I teared up. I knew I would.

They put their entire trust in me and were doing the impossible. Against medical wisdom, and self-preserving instinct, they limped along.

I watched them disappear. And then I started bawling. Hard.

Suck up the tears, babe. No jeopardizing the mission now. I had my agenda and my work cut out for me.

The plan was to get to the SUV driver's body. Hopefully they hadn't moved it, hopefully his keys were still in his pocket. Get the keys and run like I have never run to get back.

It was still lying where he died, at the bottom of the grade, surrounded by the rocks that had ended his life. I felt horrible all over again, but was relieved to see that animals hadn't found him—yet.

I had a tremendous, unintentional shiver as I patted his pockets, doing everything I could not to look at him, not to breathe in.

"Looking for these?"

My heart stopped.

Clay Hobson stood there, keys held out, jingling slightly.

I had to think. Fast. I stood up, held my hands up to show I meant no harm. "I'm just trying to get my daughter and get out of here. I know my husband did things! I know that now! I wanted the keys to drive me and my daughter to the police station!"

They stayed still. I expected more smooth talking from Clay, but he was simply standing there, staring at me.

It was the other guy who spoke first. Which was odd. *He* was odd. Agitated.

He turned to Clay and said, "She's lying." Then he turned to me and said, "You're lying!" He aimed his rifle right at me.

But Clay chimed in. "Terrence!" I hoped, his way of saying *don't.*

"Get on your knees!" he shouted at me, his rifle emphasizing his fury. He was thrusting it toward me, like a jab with an invisible bayonet. "On! Your! Knees!"

While Terrence kept his gun aimed, Clay made a show of slinging his rifle onto his back. I kept my hands halfway up. I absolutely did not want to provoke unnecessary bullets in my direction. No, thank you. My hands were going to remain very visible.

"Don't shoot her, Terrence," said Clay, calmly, authoritatively.

"Then tell her not to move."

"Miranda?" said Clay. "Nice to meet you face to face. Please don't move."

"I won't," I said, beginning to kneel. "My husband is mortally wounded. I'm here to negotiate. In fact..." I cleared my throat. "I already have a proposition that you won't want to refuse."

"Liar!" said Terrence, who was clearly on edge.

"Relax, Terrence," said Clay.

"I'm on your team, Miranda," he said. "I'm willing to compromise in every way possible. But I need you to take me to Aaron first. That's the only condition on my end.

"The reason is timing. We don't have time," Clay continued. "No, wait, let me rephrase that. Your husband doesn't have time. As you said, he's mortally wounded. I need him to be alive to fight the good fight. And you need him alive because he's the father of your child."

There was no way I could take Clay with me to Aaron. I'd be powerless if something went wrong.

"He needs a doctor," I said.

"She doesn't trust you, Clayton," murmured Terrence.

"She's a wise woman," said Clay, looking directly at me. Talking about me while talking *to* me. "She needs me to convince her."

He held his knife outward for me to see it. It looked like he was going to lay it down as a peace offering.

He raised his knife. He was behind Terrence, so it almost looked like he was going to poke him with it. For just a half second, I wondered if he would, a delirious thought. Because that would make no sense at all.

Yet that is exactly what he did.

Clay Hobson plunged his knife into the neck of his partner.

CHAPTER 19

TERRENCE SLUMPED FORWARD onto his knees. I didn't move. I didn't scream. All I could do was stare as a large stream of dark red liquid began to cascade down his chest, shining in the sunlight.

I was still down, so now the two of us were kneeling mere yards away, facing each other, like some sort of bizarre warrior ritual. The blade was lodged. As Terrence reached back to grab the handle, he found that he couldn't even raise his arms. All he could do was look at me. Toward me.

Why?

Clay must have seen it on my face. *Why did you stab your friend?*

"To protect you," answered Clay without my asking.

He stepped forward and withdrew the blade from Terrence's neck. I was watching close, petrified. He looked up and held my gaze. Then he seemed to recognize my fear and tossed it on the ground, seemingly in demonstration of a truce.

"I never wanted it to come to this," he said. He was about to bare his soul. I could feel it. "Sadly, these are the forces we're up against."

Exhibit A. He gestured toward Terrence's body. Exhibit B. The body of the SUV driver. Exhibit C. The body floating down the river.

"Aaron and I..." he said. "We're facing powers well beyond our control. I had to find the right moment. Terrence wanted to kill you, and I desperately needed to protect Aaron."

I was trembling. "W-what is this?" I asked, referring to the entirety of the debacle. The company. The men. My husband. The history. Everything.

"There isn't time," he replied. "We have to hurry."

Terrence was on the ground, facedown. It was over for him.

I felt sick, despite the fact that this wasn't even the first dead body I'd seen on this wonderful vacation. Clay used a booted foot to push him over, and it rolled with a strange limpness. There's something rather vacant about a corpse, the way the shoulder flops over. The feet surrender. The expressionless face.

Clay kneeled, inspecting the body. I doubted it was

easy for him to do what he did, but it was hard to detect telltale signs of a conscience in Clay. He seemed fine.

He looked over to tell me the heavy words I knew were eventually coming.

"Aaron's not innocent."

I didn't have a response.

"But he's a good man," he continued. "And you'll need my help if you want to bring him to a doctor."

He let that sit for a second. He stood up. *Need his help? His help?* I was suspicious but I knew I had no choice.

"A doctor?" I questioned.

"The clock's ticking."

I had to oblige him. In all these outlandish happenings, it made sense that the only way out was an outlandish offer.

"All right," I said. "But on one condition."

"Name it."

"The keys to the SUV…I carry them."

He dug in his pocket and tossed them to me. No hesitation. He was willing to do whatever I wanted.

I had more to say, more to demand. "The rifle…I hold it."

There was a natural pause here but I hit him with a third condition before he could object.

"And you…" I said. "You keep in front of me."

He weighed his options, looking across the canyon and the river, with so many nooks and crannies where one might hide. He stepped forward, closer to me but not intrusively so. I nodded to the river. He seemed to know immediately what I meant. We'd be hiking upstream.

I slung the rifle over my shoulder. The upper hand was mine now. It was tangible. Not because of the weapon, but because of the map in my head.

"Let's go," I said to him.

"Let's go save lives," he said back.

CHAPTER 20

I GUIDED CLAY through the canyon without saying anything other than where to turn. Dark thoughts were swarming around my soul like flies on a carcass. Aaron isn't innocent. Aaron may have hurt people. Aaron hid something.

"Veer toward the crest," I said to Clay.

You start a marriage with two eyes open, you stay in it with one eye closed. This is the standard advice. Yet had I proceeded along with *both* eyes closed? Was I also wearing earplugs? And a sensory deprivation suit? Did I know my husband at all?

I finally spoke up about a half hour into our hike. "Okay, fine, let's hear it," I said. "What sort of cataclysmic thing could you and Aaron be involved in?" I had a thousand questions, but needed to ask him things without *telling* him things.

"Oil," replied Clay.

We were hiking across the eastern vista, in the midst

of the most spectacular sedimentary erosion I'd ever seen. Everything out here looked like a beautiful forgery of the Grand Canyon. If only I were in a place to enjoy it.

"Oil," I scoffed.

"The answer to ninety-nine out of a hundred questions."

"Is money."

"Is oil," he insisted.

My rifle was pointed at his back. I know there's safety protocol to weapons and triggers and where you aim, but I was done being safe. If I accidentally tripped on a pebble and shot him in the spinal cord, so be it. I'd apologize in the eulogy.

"Did your husband ever tell you about the case of *Drake v. Llorenzo*?"

"No."

"That family?"

"No."

"From the town of Chasm? *Drake v. Llorenzo*? He really never told you?"

"Keep facing forward."

I was lying. Aaron had told me, but I wasn't intending to trust Clay yet. I needed to keep my guard up. Both verbally and physically.

"Llorenzo's family got long-term illnesses by a water

supply polluted by fracking," he said. "Drake Oil's fracking lines."

It was a legendary litigious nightmare spanning years. Clay knew every nuance of it and retold the chronology well enough for me to believe he was at least *part* of Aaron's legal department, or had been well briefed. The trial controversially ended when the Llorenzo family was exposed for taking bribes from a rival corporation. Another oil company was bribing Llorenzo to fabricate the entire lawsuit. The whole case was exposed as a lie. That was the brilliant Drake defense team at work. That's what won.

"I don't see how this is news," I replied when he finished.

"Ah, okay, good. So you're up to date," said Clay. "So what you probably *don't* know...what Aaron probably *hasn't* told you...is that those bribes never happened."

"You mean Drake fabricated the bribes?"

"Drake fabricated the *family*."

He was no longer the requisite twelve feet ahead of me on the trail. I'd dropped my guard. I'd completely lost focus on our spacing.

Fabricated the family?

"I don't get it," I said to him.

"Our legal team found a father of three who was willing to say he was sick."

"Even though he wasn't? Sick?" This made no sense. "So Drake invented its own fake case? Against itself?"

He was walking alongside me. My gun was no longer safely defending my personal bubble. He could've easily done something to me during this time. He could've strangled me, pushed me down, and disarmed me. I'd been completely distracted by his claim.

"It's a con game," he said. "We called it a false god. You control your enemy by controlling their hero: you *create* their hero...then you humiliate their hero."

"Why?"

"So you can make sure one big case, just one, will lose exactly the way you need it to. And when that case loses, it sets a precedent for all other cases to lose. It sways public opinion. It sways juries. It's unstoppable."

"How would you pull that off?"

"Pay everyone. Pay opposing lawyers. Pay the clerks. The cops. Judges. The hardest judge is the first one. But once a few are in, the pressure to conform is enormous. And contagious." Then he looked over at my face to mention something he knew would jar it. "Like the bonus Aaron got last year. The $145,000."

He saw me react. I tried to stay unperturbed. But the mention of that $145,000 wasn't easy to hide.

"Then what does that make *us?*" I said, half rhetorically. "What does that make you?"

"Drake is a monster. I work for them. So…" Then came an honest, grave, uninflected admission. "I'm a monster. Aaron isn't."

He talked a good game. Too good. His spin was so potent I didn't even care if he was conning me anymore.

"But I'm trying to makes amends," he added. "I'm here to help him. I was lucky to be recruited on this hunt but not lucky enough to be put in charge of it. So I had to be patient before making a move."

I decided to take a risk. "Who's Jed?"

He scrutinized me again. The gears turning in his head.

"You mean Jedediah," he said. "He's a retired judge. Drake has leases on his property for some of our fracking sites."

"So Jed is helping," I concluded.

"No, Miranda." He stopped to look me deep in the eye. "Let me make this crystal clear: you can't trust Jed."

I didn't respond. I didn't tell him to keep moving. I didn't need to. We had arrived.

We could now see the site where our minivan had crashed. All four wheels were belly-up, facing the sky. The vehicle had been drenched, jostled, twisted ten degrees, carried, scraped, then dumped back on the silt of the same bank several yards downstream.

It definitely looked like a crime scene, though.

"They were at the wreck?" asked Clay, scanning the area in front of us. "They were at the wreck the whole time?"

I kept him in front of me for the final few steps. I wanted to monitor his reactions. I wanted to see if he licked his lips with a thirst for vengeance, or was genuine in wanting to talk to Aaron.

"Here?" he asked again, almost squeaking the word. His incredulity mirrored a growing, nagging, terrifying fear that was welling up within me.

I was about to find out if they made it. If they had an accident. Or worse.

Or if they made it to the SUV, but someone was waiting for them when they got there.

CHAPTER 21

I STARTED SHOUTING for them. "Aaron! Aaaaaaarrrrron!" I repeated the refrain as I stood looking up the cliff face, looking for any signs of life.

"I thought you said he was here," said Clay.

I continued to scan the cliff, and that's when I saw it: a small purple smudge about halfway up.

"What... is... ?" I muttered to myself.

Her little kangaroo hat, lodged up in the rock. Which could only be up there if—

"Sierra!" I shouted.

Clay turned around and saw me looking up.

"Aaron!" I shouted.

"So they climbed up," said Clay. He brushed past me, leaving me in his dust.

He was already on his way.

I ran after him. Soon I was ahead of him. He chose one route. I chose the other. Within minutes we were vertical. I tried to peer downward, directly along the vertical face to inspect the long, thin pocket space that ran along the foothills.

"Aaron!" I shouted upward, past Clay, into the elongated void.

No response.

Clay didn't stop, and soon our two routes began to converge. They started out parallel but around the halfway point they angled into each other. He wouldn't look at me. You'd think it was the shame of knowing he'd betrayed me, but I caught sight of a cocky smile.

Without even glancing over he said, "You're not gonna get there before me, Miranda," he said.

He was a genuine climber, too. Perhaps better than I was.

"If you were *really* an ally," I replied, "you'd call out for him."

I started to outpace my rival. I was taking more chances than he was, reaching for holds beyond my normal span. But Clay kept up.

"You're not calling out to him," I continued, "because you don't want him to know that you're with me."

I was gradually forming a new theory. I didn't think Mr. Clay Hobson was simply ordered to do the job of attacking my husband. I didn't think this entire day was merely an assignment. The truth was that my nemesis, hovering twenty feet to my seven o'clock, was directly implicated in whatever ugly history they all shared. This wasn't a job—it was personal.

"Aaron!" I again shouted upward. "Run!"

CHAPTER 22

I WAS ABOUT fifteen feet ahead of Clay. I would have to use that advantage as soon as I reached the top. If only I had some hot water or oil.

He wasn't taking any chances. He freed up his right hand, pried loose a small rock, and threw it at me. I thought there was no way it'd actually—

"Ow!" I screamed, as the rock hissed into my hand.

He'd tagged me directly on the knuckles. A one-in-a-hundred shot. The pain was instant, loosening my grip, but it was a miss for my opponent. He was aiming for my head.

I looked down toward him. Thirty feet behind me now—but he'd chosen his route badly and had hit a dead end. He'd have to go down and over to my route and, maybe in a few minutes catch up with me. But he readied another rock to throw.

I had the rifle on my back. I remembered when I fired it into the air, the recoil. My shoulder was still sore. If

I tried shooting it now, it would knock me off the wall. Thinking about the gun, I lost concentration, promptly losing the foothold under my left toe.

I started to fall.

I swung half a pendulum arc, my body anchored only by my middle three fingers on my right hand as I lost three of my four holds. Pebbles crumbled from where my feet were, a hundred feet down to the crevasse below me. My rifle strap slid off my shoulder, down my torso, past my legs, and sailed toward the abyss, ricocheting off the cliff face, past where Clay might have caught it midair—no chance, although he did try—before spinning into the trench below.

We both paused for a moment.

He broke the silence. "Let's stop and think, Miranda. I believe we may have a misunderstanding."

I could see the look in his eyes. There was no misunderstanding. He was a demonic tarantula crawling up from below relentlessly. I'd originally thought we were evenly matched. I was wrong. He was immensely better at this. He had chosen a bad route, but was now rushing up behind me with a violent focus.

Bloodlust.

Then he made a move I didn't see coming.

"Aaron!" he yelled upward.

What is he doing?

"Aaron Cooper!" he yelled again.

I kept climbing.

"Your wife is coming to kill you, Aaron!"

What?!

"She thinks you betrayed her!"

He's insane. Did he actually think this would work? I started accelerating my climb even faster than its already uncomfortable speed. I took risks that required not looking down. "Don't listen to him!" I shouted upward.

"She's lost her mind, Aaron!" he yelled. "Protect Sierra! Because Miranda is coming to kill you!"

My husband would never believe this. Though, in his delirious state...I scrambled over the edge in an ungraceful lunge, then stood by the road getting my bearings. I grabbed the purple kangaroo hat. My predator was no more than thirty seconds behind me on the trek. I'd need every nanosecond of that margin.

Go!

The black SUV was parked down the road. I vaulted the guardrail and sprinted directly for it. I was of course profoundly relieved to see it there, but also instantly reminded that this vehicle was the source of my misery.

No matter, it was a sight for sore eyes. This model

came with all the options I ever wanted: Aaron and Sierra!

As I got closer, stumbling my last few steps, I could see the two of them lying against the rear wheel. When I sent them up here, it had seemed impossible. I don't know if I actually believed they could make it. But there they were, delivered as promised. One napping daughter and one still-intact husband.

"Get inside!" I shouted at them. *"Get inside!"*

Clay was just making his way over the guardrail, only ten seconds behind me. I fumbled for the keys and the unlock button. Aaron and Sierra started to stir, roused by my voice, but gradually, too gradually for my liking. I arrived like a train wreck, my own momentum slamming me against the rear door on the driver's side. I yanked it open to shove (as gently as I could) the wobbling Aaron into the interior, throwing Sierra in his lap. I flung open the driver's door and jumped in, cranking the ignition just as the rear window was shattered.

Clay had found a rock—probably forged from his own kidney stones—to smash the window. He was already thrusting his arms into the backseat, attempting to grab my husband by the collar.

"Daddy!" cried Sierra, seeing her father about to get yanked into the clutches of pure evil.

I stomped on the gas and gunned it. Clay's arms retreated as the SUV rocketed forward, and we finally hit the road at full speed. I wanted to make Clay appear in my rearview mirror and shrink.

And he did. Just as two white vans emerged in the distance behind him. His reinforcements.

CHAPTER 23

THE SPEED LIMIT was fifty on this treacherous desert road. I was doing eighty-five. Barely paying attention to handling the turns, I only cared about making the little white dots in my rearview mirror shrink.

Both vans had stopped to pick up their overlord, then quickly regained their cruising speed. I was mesmerized by the rearview mirror. I lost focus on the road before I corrected my swerve, fishtailed a bit, and steadied. *Miranda, you've officially been issued a second chance to get this right.*

To steer into the skid.

I banked hard on the next turn. It was a tight enough curve that it was marked with a road sign in cautionary yellow. SPEED LIMIT 45 MPH.

I took it at a hundred.

The back tires squealed as our entire SUV tilted toward the cliff. Not decisively so, but enough for me to dig my fingernails into the supple, calfskin, optional leather-covered steering wheel.

The white vans weren't slowing down at all. In fact, the closer one was a turn behind me as we slalomed along the S-curves.

"Hold on tight, please," I said to my cargo.

I lowered my glance at the rearview mirror to peek into the backseat at Aaron. He looked sickly pale, his skin was a blank, white canvas for a wife's deepest fears.

"I'm gonna find us a hospital," I said to him.

I started fumbling for the air-conditioning switch. These brand new SUVs have monstrously elaborate control panels. It looked like NASA in there. Temperature. Humidity. Angle. Dual. Custom.

"Babe, there's gotta be a bottle of water somewhere."

He didn't answer. There was an orange backpack on the seat next to me, which I started to dig through, filled with hard paper rods. No water.

"Babe?" I said.

"I can find it, Mommy," Sierra spoke up.

Before I could caution her not to roam the interior of a vehicle that's careening around cliff roads, she was up and about, crawling over the headrest, so that her tiny bottom filled my rearview mirror for a moment. And just behind her, flying out of the previous turn we just finished, I could see something terrifying.

The first white van. Directly behind us. With passengers. With guns.

My hand fumbled across the air-conditioning panel, inadvertently scraping the radio volume knob upward. I grabbed the wheel with both hands and floored it, as music started blaring—Johnny Cash's "Ring of Fire"—while our SUV roared down the road at one hundred five miles per hour.

We thoroughly skidded at *every* turn. The back of the vehicle fishtailed and I'd correct it by guiding the front wheels toward the potential danger. It worked. We stayed in control.

But so did the white vans, who apparently had less to lose than we did, because they both dared every law of physics. Every maneuver, every curve—they were gaining on us.

And soon they were on either side.

"Mommy!"

Out came those guns. On my left, a man leaned out of the passenger window, wielding a nasty-looking contraption that fired more bullets than I ever wanted to know about.

BRATATATATAT! Either it was a warning shot or his aim was bad, but I could see the bullets whiz by in front of my windshield, and I didn't want to find out.

I'm sure the best move would've been to slam on my brakes and have him magically end up shooting the other van. That's how it works in cartoons, but I'm just not that kind of animated rabbit. Instead I jolted the steering wheel sharply to the left and slammed our SUV against the passenger door he was shooting from.

We bounced into the van and would've lost control had I not escalated the maneuver by swerving back across the road into the other guy for stabilization.

Wham!

Our SUV thus corrected its course and remained centered down the stretch of road, as the vehicles on either side of me lost traction. The first van wiggled, slowing him down so he was now slightly behind us; the other scraped the rock face and, to my shock and delight, careened back into the first one.

Now the two vans were meeting in my rearview mirror. And at a hundred miles per hour, that wasn't a simple collision.

This would buy us at least five minutes.

I sped up to one hundred twenty-five miles per hour. I had to assume they'd resume the chase, if they could, when they could. I didn't know what the capacity of my engine was but I knew my tires were shaking. Big, oafish SUVs are not meant to go *triple* the speed limit. Yet, miraculously, within a few minutes we were emerging out of the canyons, beginning the hundred-mile downslope back toward civilization. I still shook with adrenaline, constantly checking my rearview mirror as the mountains gave way to hills and landscape broadened to wide-open space.

Finally arriving at the closest intersection with the highway, I saw a flimsy barricade shutting down access to the opposite lane. No wonder! This was already a desolate highway, but Clay had ensured total privacy.

"Mommy, this is water," said Sierra. She'd found a bottle, half full with its lovely, clear contents.

"Thanks, honey. Back in your seat. We're safe."

We weren't safe, yet. We still had to encounter our first normal human. The road ahead remained sparse, mile after mile. Empty. But I needed her to hear those words. And I needed to say them.

We needed a doctor, but also needed protection. Clay said not to trust Jed, and we obviously could not trust Clay, and Aaron said be careful who you trust, so I had no idea what else was in store.

As the land opened up I could finally see my way ahead. There were roadside stores, gas stations, signs of civilization, and finally a sign for a town: Chasm, Arizona. I knew it had a population of maybe a couple thousand people, seemingly spread throughout the hills on either side of the highway.

I was driving us to the only location I knew of. Our original destination before all this started. Jed's ranch.

CHAPTER 24

"SALVATION," I SAID to Aaron in the backseat.

He stirred.

We pulled into Jed's ranch, which was easy to find because it was the only settlement for miles. I remember how isolated it had looked on our map when we started the drive—what seemed like ten years ago.

There were two small oil derricks just inside the front gate. We drove in with a flurry of dust behind us, barely slowing down for the turn.

"Plant," he murmured.

"That's right, babe. We found it."

"I'm…I'm…" he said with slurred speech. "Plant."

He must've been delusional at this point. Sweaty. Dehydrated. He was incoherently pointing at the oil wells.

The ranch property was massive, deep enough that the front drive alone ran a half mile. Once in the main roundabout, there was a barn, a shed, a small industrial-looking building, a house, and five or six different oil derricks strewn across the hillside.

I drove straight for the house and screeched to a stop by the porch. I grabbed Sierra and clutched her to my chest.

"Aaron, I need to go find a phone. Or a human being. You're allowed to pass out once you're in an ambulance, okay? No passing out before that, okay?"

"Plant," he said. Again.

I kissed his knee, the closest thing I could access while holding our child and trying not to waste precious seconds. Then I hurried toward the main house. There was a pickup truck parked out front. Shiny, new. Even in my hurry, I couldn't help but notice how nice the porch was.

"Hello?" I hollered. I walked up to the front door and rang the bell.

"My name is Miranda. Hello?! Jedediah? Can you call 911?"

I rang it again. I waited an agonizing five seconds. Then I tried the knob, felt it turn, thank God, and opened the door.

"Hello! Jed?" I said again. I walked in. I could apologize later.

The house was big and pleasant. And devoid of people. No radio playing. No pasta steaming on the stove in the back.

"Anybody home?"

"Anybody home?" echoed Sierra, my assistant.

We crept in and wandered all the way to the back without seeing a single soul. We crossed a long hallway leading to the rear of the house. The place was immaculate. More like a museum than a residence. Everything was untouched.

In what looked like a sitting room, I saw a phone. A land line.

I rushed the last few steps to snatch it up. I must have dialed 911 about five times in a row before I truly listened to the receiver. It was dead. No hiss. No tone.

"Dead?" I exclaimed, turning to look around. *What's up with this place?* Panic began to set in.

Then I heard a clunk.

It came from the far end of the house. Some shuffling, then another clunk. Somebody was opening drawers in a desk. Opening and slamming. Somebody was in a hurry.

"Hello?" I said again. "Jedediah?" I went toward the shuffling noise.

From the hallway, I saw him. He was standing right there. A big, grizzly man, with white hair. His back was to me. He didn't turn around.

None of this felt right. None of this looked right,

smelled right, sounded right. He'd have to have heard me yelling in his house a moment ago, but seemed unaware of my presence.

I was far enough away to do the following. Based on pure instinct, I quietly turned to Sierra and I gestured *shhh.* She complied, seeing the look on my face. I nudged her gently toward the side room right beside me, a hiding spot.

Then the homeowner turned around and looked squarely at me. His expression was not friendly. Neither was the shotgun he was holding down by his side.

I was tired of meeting men in this way. That *this town ain't big enough for the two of us* macho manure. We should've hugged each other and danced around the living room in circles—that's how I'd pictured this meeting. But he was silent.

"Are you Jed?" I asked. "I'm Aaron Cooper's wife. I'm Miranda."

He was just watching me. Cold.

"C-can..." I stuttered. "Can I use your phone?"

He muttered, "Don't have one."

He doesn't have a phone?

"Look," I said. "I'm sorry to intrude. There's no need for a gun. Do you have a cell phone I could use? Aaron is hurt. Badly. Can you help me find Jed?"

He kept looking down at me. He stood six foot three,

easily. Viking big. An older man, but one who could torque a lug nut with his bare hands.

What was he doing? My husband was going to die. We didn't have another house we could get to soon enough. We didn't have anyone else we could trust.

And then I looked behind him and noticed a phone line on the wall.

The line was cut. Severed. A fresh incision that wasn't made last year or last month; it was made two minutes ago. He saw me see it. He now knew that I knew that he wasn't a nice person.

He said, "I *am* Jed."

CHAPTER 25

JED HEADED FOR the front door. With his shotgun. Toward the SUV. Toward Aaron. "No!" I shouted. "Wait!"

He didn't stop. I knew he would figure out where Aaron was, if he hadn't already.

I felt helpless. I needed a gun. For someone who'd never even *held* a gun prior to yesterday, I certainly got addicted fast.

I picked up Sierra, moving her to safety and looking for the gun rack I knew had to be in the house somewhere. None in this room. None in the hallway.

"Can you wait for me here?" I said to Sierra.

"Yes, Mommy."

No weapons in the living room. My panic tripled. "Are you my little angel?"

"I'm your Mister."

"My...?" I asked, kicking open a back room door.

"Mister," she repeated. "Of Transportation."

She made me want to weep like a spigot. "Yes! I'll be right back, okay? I need to help Daddy."

Running to the kitchen for a knife, I looked out through the living room window and saw that Jed was already at the SUV.

"Aaron!" I screamed. It was like a TV screen whose channel couldn't be changed. I froze.

Jed had his shotgun aimed as he crept forward the last few steps to the car. The tinted window was up on this side of the vehicle, meaning he couldn't see inside, but he held his gun aimed directly at the backseat.

With no warning, *blam blam!,* he blasted two shots in through the window.

"No!" I screamed.

He yanked open the door. I could see directly into the backseat where Aaron would be.

Where Aaron wasn't.

Jed was looking at an empty backseat. He leaned in to check the rear compartment, came back out and looked around. The structures on the ranch were spread out, with not many places to hide.

Where was my husband?! That was the pertinent question.

And then we got our answer.

Boom!

What sounded like a building being *thrown* into

another building was actually a fiery explosion big and bright enough that even in the middle of the Arizona daylight, you could see the flash, toward the main gate. A fireball the size of a warehouse had just plumed. The derrick underneath it was now a geyser of fire.

Aaron apparently knows his way around an oil well.

CHAPTER 26

JED STOOD THERE gawking at the spectacle. It was nice to see someone else caught off guard for a change.

Then he started heading toward the mayhem, a man on a mission.

To whatever degree he'd previously wanted Aaron dead, it was imperative now. I saw him cock his shotgun as he stomped toward the flaming derrick. I frantically ran back through the house. If I hurried, I could intercept Jed.

I imagined Aaron would've set off the explosion, then hobbled over to some bush to collapse. I sprinted through the house and burst through the back door.

And that was as far as I'd have to go to collide with the love of my life.

Aaron and I banged into each other head first and both grunted.

"You... But... Which... Did...?"

"How...? I... If..."

Then I kissed him.

Passionately. Both of my hands gripping his collar. My body pressed against his. Which felt way better than I'll ever admit in a court of law.

Then we got down to business. He had the orange backpack from the SUV. Those rods I saw earlier—*duh, Miranda*—were sticks of dynamite. Should've known.

"Fear is an amazing motivator," he said.

"I thought that guy was a friend. That's Jed. Jed Branch. But we need to get out of here as fast as—"

He took a step forward then lurched and lowered himself to the ground. I crouched beside him immediately. "Aaron!"

"I'm…I'm so sorry," he said, the adrenaline wearing off, barely able to speak. "Last year I found…puzzle pieces…people getting sick, families asking questions. By the time this…this…awful picture emerged…they were killing anyone who knew even one percent of it. I couldn't risk…letting anyone know that I knew. Which meant…trying to protect you by…" He started to tear up. "By keeping it from you."

I had to get him out of here. But how?

"Babe, *babe,* listen." I had to keep him rational. "I know you did right by us. You're a good soul. You don't have to prove anything to me."

"No, that's my point," he said. He pulled me close

enough to whisper urgently, which we didn't have time for and he knew it. "What I'm telling you is, I'm truly sorry."

"Aaron."

"For keeping you in the dark." His tears were streaming hard, nearly re-energizing him. "I was too scared...of how many people were tied to it. But that's no excuse. I was getting set to blow the whistle. I was. Today in fact. At a labor strike here on the ranch. But I needed to hide you and Sierra. And Jed was the only ally. But Jed's actually...Jed's actually..."

An evil, backstabbing worm? I knew what he wanted to call Jed. I'd already met several members of his species this morning.

"Babe," I said, pulling him up to his feet. "You did something I could never hold against you....You tried to keep our family safe. So now...if I get us through this day...we'll be even."

He hugged me. I was about to bawl. The hurricane of emotions was finally catching up to me. And he felt so good to hold. But this wasn't the moment.

"Now, we need to get out of here." I grabbed his hand and hurried him to the back. We burst in on Sierra, who instantly perked up. "Mommy! Daddy!" I already knew what must be done, and there wasn't a moment to spare. I grabbed his orange backpack.

"Wha…?" he said.

"Where is that labor strike?" I asked.

I loved his move of lighting up the derrick. It was a gargantuan middle finger to Jedediah. It was a brilliant way to create chaos. And, most of all, it was a beacon. Of hope. That fireball and its smoke, and now its continual fountain of flames, would be visible for miles around—in particular, for whoever was at the rally.

"Not far—on the other side of the canyon. Behind the ranch."

There were other derricks on this ranch, just up the hillside. While Jed would be dousing the rig that was on fire, I could ignite another, and then another, one by one, making my way toward the strike. Help was sure to come. It might not be an ambulance at first, but it would be somebody.

Bag in hand, I started heading out.

"Where are you going?" asked Aaron.

"To finish what you started."

CHAPTER 27

IF I COULD avoid the wide-open stretch between the main house and the barn, somehow dart between the trees or sneak behind the random tractors parked along the road, I could survive the trip.

But Jedediah was already returning with his shotgun.

I ran to the first outer corner of the house, then peered around the edge to monitor him. The hope was for my dear husband to find a new hiding place so that Jedediah, or whoever came next, wouldn't get to him so fast.

Uh-oh. Down the long drive, the white vans were roaring into the ranch, dust rising behind them. Both battered vehicles came to a halt in the middle of the courtyard. "Whoever came next" was here.

Jedediah arrived as men jumped out—six, by my count—including Clay.

That was my cue. While they were distracted, I sprinted up the back area, up into the hillside toward the cluster of derricks.

These two days had taken their toll on my legs: they were now Jell-O, buckling beneath every step. But I didn't have the luxury of indulging in weakness. *Push, Mandy.*

Too many minutes later, I tumbled forward into a helpful ditch, then turned around to spy on the activity. Far below, the group had begun to disperse. I'd glanced backward midway through my run, catching glimpses of the men arming themselves with rifles and pistols, Jedediah in charge. He and Clay were gesturing around, probably cataloging all the places I could be hiding. But they deployed their legion of thugs toward the main house.

Where Aaron and Sierra were.

"Do not go in there," I muttered quietly through clenched teeth.

Time to move. I hustled over to the first derrick, twice as big as it looked from afar. A colossal robot arm angrily punching mother earth. I was only too happy to fish out my first stick of dynamite. I drew on years of fieldwork to calculate the most vulnerable spot.

Ten seconds later—*boom!*

I'd gotten clear but it was deafening. The blast knocked me over, flat on my face, welcoming me to the earth I was avenging. I rose to my hands and knees to look down the slope into the heart of the ranch. All seven gentlemen were now looking back up toward my handiwork. Good.

There were some shouts and gesticulations, then they started coming my way.

Bring it.

I wanted them to march up the hill. All of them at once. I could just run like a rabbit, deeper into the property, toward the derricks, toward the labor strike itself. The first explosion was several minutes ago. Whoever was over at the factory had to have heard something by now, and seen the smoke.

The thug team was getting its fresh orders from Jed. Jed was indeed in charge. Which meant Clay had played me well. *Don't trust Jed, Miranda.* He knew that if he lost my confidence, I'd run to whomever he'd told me *not* to trust. And I did just that. Right into his crystal-clear trap.

But Jed and Clay seemed to be arguing. Then, abruptly, most of the men were sent in the other direction, back into the ranch—all, in fact, except Clay.

Clay was coming toward me. *Alone.* Which meant he took this personally.

That made two of us.

CHAPTER 28

CLAY CAME HUSTLING up the hill, frothing at the mouth. There was no question he fueled the vengeance in this troop. If Jedediah was the brain, Clay was the bile duct.

"You're dead!" he shouted outward.

He didn't know exactly where I was. I'd been squatting behind a clump of brush and cacti. He was trying to flush me out.

"Miranda!" he roared.

Another game of Marco Polo, hoping I'd bite the worm on the hook. I didn't. He had his own explosives now. Two sticks from Jed. The one way to extinguish oil fires is to blow them up.

The next derrick on my demolition list was way up the ridge, making for a long sprint along a trench in the hillside. I waited for the right moment, then ran for it.

Crack, crack, crack! Gunshots chased right after me. Clay wasn't fooling around anymore. He wanted me erased.

I kept going, running and running, eventually and unexpectedly reaching a barbed-wire fence. Was this it? Was this the rally? I could see a number of industrial derricks and a factory. This wasn't Jedediah's property anymore. This was the edge of Drake's northernmost fracking plant.

And now the closest well was a fracking rig. A big, metallic mosquito of human engineering, sticking its snout deep and horizontal into its victim to slurp a mile sideways.

There was indeed a crowd in the distance. The labor strike! My first glimpse of normal people. Maybe a hundred of them.

"Help!" I shouted toward them. *"Help!"*

But they were too far away to hear me and were all gazing about ninety degrees in another direction, toward the last explosion I made, which was an understandably enticing thing to gaze at.

I'd have to lure them with another boom.

I ran for the closest well. *Crack,* another bullet ripped through the air, close enough that I actually heard it swish by my head. I arrived at the rig and dove for cover under the web of its piping. I soon had the dynamite sticks nestled in the crook of the main tube.

And that's when I was hit from behind.

Jed. The butt of his shotgun.

I'd been spared the bullets because he didn't want to aim toward explosives and high-pressure flammable gas.

But Jed didn't factor in how hard I'd hit him back. This gal had grown with the fight. Nothing could faze me at this point.

I spun around and rammed him head first, nailing him square in the midsection. He was a big guy, but his age had caught up to him. Chugging up the hillside left him vulnerable.

He went down hard and I quickly straddled his oily torso and started punching him with all my might. Over and over. Left, right, left.

Which is when a few members of the crowd emerged over the crest of the hill. And the first thing they saw was me beating up an old, gray-haired man. Which they certainly didn't let go unchecked.

"Hey, get off him!" said one of the workers.

"Hey, she's beating on someone!" said another.

Clay arrived just in time to ruin any chance for truth to prevail.

"This is your arsonist!" said Clay, pointing at me.

"Wait," I protested.

But the crowd was gathering and opinions were forming fast.

"This is the arsonist," one of the workers shouted

back to the others. Someone had keys to the gate in the fence and opened it up right away.

Clay capitalized on the chaos. "She's got the fuses for the dynamite in her front pocket! Look! And the igniter in her right fist. Look!"

The crowd was looking at me. I was so out of breath I could barely speak.

"That's not…that's not true," I said.

"He's right," said a woman with tattooed forearms. "She's got fuse wire."

"No, I mean…it's not true that I'm the…that I'm the…" I couldn't finish my sentence. I had reached my absolute mental and physical limit.

Clay was in full force, grandstanding to the gathering crowd. "This woman has been trying to start fires all along the canyon. *On the day of your rally!* You tell me—is that a coincidence?"

More and more people were gathering.

Clay continued. "Your families, your friends, all conveniently clustered in one vulnerable location."

The crowd was growing hostile. There were awful names being shouted at me. This was their day to vent frustration, and now, thanks to Clay, this was their day to route it toward me.

I tried to step away from the growing circle.

"Not goin' anywhere, miss," said a man in a cowboy

hat, rifle in hand. Folks in this part of the universe carried guns. Proudly.

"Please," I implored them. "I need to call an ambulance. My husband needs an ambulance."

"Stop lying!" said Clay.

"Yeah," said a worker, joining in the mob mentality. "Stop lying."

"She's a radical!" said Clay. "Hired by Drake to sabotage the strike!"

I started to struggle against the grip of the crowd but more and more people were shoving me back to the center. The two fires roared behind me.

After all I'd been through—was this really how I was going to go out?

The chorus of discontented voices grew and grew until someone said, "Kill her."

And someone else shouted, *"No, you kill me first!"*

CHAPTER 29

AND THAT CHANGED everything.

It was a thunderous voice, slightly ragged, but resounding with confidence and conviction that I've only heard emanate from one person. My husband.

"Me first!" roared Aaron. "Kill me first!"

The crowd all stopped. Hushed itself. They slowly opened their ranks to let him take center stage. He had Sierra in his arms. Knees buckling as he walked, he'd expended his last breath to walk up the hillside.

"Me...not her," he said one last time.

He knew what he was doing—the locals reacted instantly.

"Aaron Cooper," said the woman with the forearm tattoos, as if his name were holy.

"It *is* him," said someone else with equal awe. "It *is* Aaron."

They couldn't believe what they were seeing. I couldn't

either. Whatever it was. Him. Their savior. He stood in the middle, commanding all their attention, all their respect.

"This is my wife," he said. "Her name is Miranda. Today she faced a monster. And that monster…that monster is standing right next to her."

"Quiet!" shouted Clay. Then he addressed the crowd. "You can't trust him!"

"Clay and his cronies rammed us off the road," continued Aaron, pointing at Clay. "Then he tried to kill her. Then, when he knew he couldn't cover any of it up, he had Jed try to kill all of us."

"This man is a liar!" said Clay, pointing his finger back at my husband.

"This man is Aaron Cooper!" said a woman from the back.

She had a small child with her. She nodded toward Aaron like he was her favorite brother. "He's defending my home and my family." Then she turned to Clay. "I'd trust him over you." Then she nodded to Jed to add, "Over both of you!"

"So would I," said another local.

"So would I," said another.

"Aaron Cooper's been helping us for almost a year," said the guy in the cowboy hat. "I'd trust him with the life of my newborn."

The workers and residents had taken his side, our side, which felt amazing, truly.

I finally spoke up. "I can tell you what this man did. I can tell you every detail."

Clay had reached his threshold. With the flames of hell whipping around behind him, he aimed his rifle directly at my chest and shouted his war cry, *"Liar!"*

I saw each split-second elapse individually. I heard each millimeter of his index finger begin to pull that sliver of metal. A flurry of gunshots went off. And I swear I felt each bullet go inside me.

CHAPTER 30

BUT THAT WAS an illusion. The others fired, Aaron's defenders and now mine. A total of fifteen rounds from four different guns. I don't think anyone missed. Every single shot pierced Clay Hobson in the chest before he ever squeezed his own trigger.

The bullet-riddled man teetered backward, took two clumsy steps, paused, coughed up blood, then fell into the trench behind him, into the roaring inferno of the rig, where instantly the dynamite sticks in his vest combusted.

Boom.

Luckily, our crowd was on the opposite edge of the blast radius. Clay Hobson wasn't spared. His body was obliterated, while the rest of us remained dazed but still on our feet. Aaron had instinctively clutched downward, curling himself over Sierra. She was shell-shocked, but she would see her fifth birthday.

The one person now trembling in our midst was Jedediah.

The crowd had fully aligned itself with Aaron, defending him, and thereby me. Jed's goons were nowhere to be seen, successfully evaded by my determined husband.

"Set your gun down, Jed," said the tattooed woman.

Jed didn't seem popular here. Maybe everyone saw through him.

The man in the cowboy hat cocked his revolver. "Jedediah Branch, I don't care how high you are on the food chain. If you move one molecule of that index finger, I will shoot you in the throat."

Jed was pale. He lowered his weapon slowly.

I gingerly made my way over to Aaron. I wanted so badly to hug him but he looked frail enough to crush. I didn't even want to exhale in his direction. Instead, I took my place at his side.

Jed was covered in oil, head to toe, doused by the spray of snuffing out the first derrick. One of the men looked directly at Jed, pulled out a pocket lighter and flicked it without ever breaking eye contact, holding the flame aloft like a torch.

Jed trembled in horror. The implication was terrifying. These people might actually burn him alive. He dropped to his knees, to face, of all people, Aaron.

"No. Please," Jed began to grovel. "Please don't."

He must've been convinced Aaron would condemn

him. I had to be honest: seeing my husband hold our child, thrashed, bruised, teetering on the edge of death, mere yards away from the man responsible for the agony of it all, I almost wondered if he might actually give the word.

Almost.

But I knew better. I knew what Jed didn't know.

"You asked me to speak at the rally on behalf of Drake, but you found out I was going to blow the whistle on the whole operation. So you ordered me killed. You ordered my family killed. All so you could keep getting kickbacks from Drake Oil while these laborers got sicker and sicker, poisoned by the drinking water in their own homes."

Aaron stared at Jed.

"You want me to call them off?" said Aaron to the judge.

Aaron isn't a murderer.

"I'll make you glad you did," said Jed. He kept his movements slow and cautious, well aware of the muzzles pointing at his vital organs. His desperate gaze turned to me. "Please, Miranda. Anything you want."

"There's nothing you can say," I told him.

His ghostly face then peered around the group, frantically calculating.

"I'll say it," said Jed. He took a deep breath. "I did

what you saw other judges do. I obstructed justice. I was paid to rule in favor of Drake Oil." He clasped his hands as if in prayer. Imploring. "But I can make it right. Help me make it right."

It had no value, this sad speech. Under duress, stating something he'd later dispute, it had no legal weight. This was just another stunt. But the moral victory definitely tasted sweet.

What was bizarre was that everyone was staring at me just as much as they were staring at the judge, wondering what kind of verdict *I* would render.

"Help me, Miranda," pleaded Jed.

I said, "My family will be giving you back your $145,000."

I let that sit for a second, watching his confusion.

"The bonus your people paid us?" I continued. "You'll be getting all that back. Starting with..." I began to fish in the pockets of my jeans. Here came all the cash I had on me, some bills and two coins, a grand total of six dollars and eleven cents. I tossed the wad toward Jedediah, then added, "The rest is coming soon."

In the distance were sirens.

I looked over at Aaron. He emitted a frail half chuckle, his best version of a laugh. Which meant, given the state he was in, that he found me hysterical.

"There's an ambulance for you, Mr. Cooper," said the

tattooed lady, kindly. She was pointing to the front gate at the far end of the ranch, ready to assist him down the road.

I still didn't want to hug my husband for fear of toppling him over, but before I could tell him no, he put Sierra on the ground and embraced me. Sierra glommed on to us to make it a three-way group effort. We held. We held tight.

We held our family as if we'd just learned what the word meant.

EPILOGUE

THAT DAY FELT like a year. And that's how long it would ultimately take to ram this monstrosity of a case through the Arizona court system, where Aaron had been summoned to testify, where I was now waiting out in the hallway for him.

Sierra was orbiting around the corridor like an urban tumbleweed. She'd abandoned her career in kangaroo development and moved on to portrait photography, snapping pictures of random faces wherever we went.

"There," she said, pointing into the courtroom. The door had opened briefly, giving her a glimpse of the distant witness stand and her daddy taking a seat. "Daddy! He's handsome."

She could hardly comprehend how important this was. He was about to provide landmark testimony that would essentially bury the oil titan for good. I could hardly comprehend it myself. All nine active members of the board would sink. The CEO, the previous CEO, the army of vice presidents, *Jedediah* and all the other judges who were bought off, the late Clay Hobson, everyone whose hands were dirty.

It got too much for me to watch, to be honest. The trial recognized case after case of ravaged families, and last week, while sitting in on testimony from a balding mother of three, two of whom were in caskets, I wound up getting escorted out of the room. For yelling at the defense.

I'm the reason gavels were invented.

As for Aaron's culpability, our infamous Tuesday in the canyon helped sway any public doubt as to whether we'd duly suffered. I mean, let's not forget, Aaron was the one person who tried to drown this demon the moment he learned it existed.

"Mommy, that lady is staring," said Sierra, having just snapped a photo down the hall. She leaned over to show me a woman on her screen, a woman who was now approaching in a high-heeled cadence that echoed across the marble. She was indeed staring. At me.

Soon her stilettos came to a crisp halt right in front of my chair. She was tall, tall like a statue-of-democracy tall, her business suit failing to hide a well-chiseled figure.

"Miranda Cooper," she said to me. A question with no question mark.

"Uh," I replied.

"My apologies for being abrupt. My name is Kelly Miles. I have a job offer."

"Oh."

"My team fights the kind of battles I think you'd appreciate. And we happen to need a geologist. Someone to cover the Caspian Sea. Someone like you. Someone hard to stop."

Hard to stop. Is that my new slogan?

"Ah." The only reply I could think of besides *uh* and *oh*.

She looked like she could dent a concrete wall just by glaring at it. I got the feeling she wasn't offering me a job so much as telling me she already hired me. The Caspian? Isn't that Russia? And missiles?

"I..." I didn't know what to say. "I like your...confidence...but..."

"But you're declining," she said. Another question with no question mark.

I looked over at Sierra as if she might teleprompt me. Sierra was riffling through her latest photos. Some seventy-five pictures in seventy-five seconds. No help.

"What I am is..." I said, "honored. And, yes, declining. But thank you."

She smiled. "My card." She handed me her business card. "You can throw it away as soon as I'm gone. Nice to meet you, Miranda Cooper. You did well."

She started walking away. And within ten more photos from Sierra, our strange visitor had disappeared around the corner.

I looked down. I contemplated the card. A new frontier. Wild terrain. The thrill of the hunt.

And I crumpled it up.

PLEASE HELP BEFORE HE KILLS ME.

This year, Christmas with his family isn't quite as Jon Roscoe had planned.

Read on for an extract

Chicago, Illinois

SNOW WAS FALLING AND the airport road snarled as Jon Roscoe sat cramped in the rear of a Chicago cab. As the car slowly made its way into the city's O'Hare Airport, Roscoe's mind drifted while he gazed through the window at the wintery scene. Imagining the delight his twin daughters would find in the falling flakes, his own heart sank as the traffic ground almost to a halt. All he wanted was to be back home in London with his family.

His car crawled forward in front of terminal buildings and as it did so, Roscoe's attention was drawn to a news story running on the in-cab TV.

'This is Katie Coakley from outside the Cook County Criminal Courthouse,' began the reporter, 'where late last night the manslaughter trial of Matteo Ginevra, son of multimillionaire construction magnate Enzo Ginevra, collapsed sensationally after lead prosecution witness Jerry Davis, a former employee of Tribeca Luxury Hotels, recanted his earlier evidence.

'Davis had previously testified to the Chicago PD to witnessing Matteo Ginevra force two construction workers to ride unsecured on a steel girder, as it was hoisted over fifty floors during the building of the Chicago Tribeca Luxury Hotel. Davis had also testified to Ginevra's appearing intoxicated by liquor while on the construction site.

'Yesterday evening he amended his evidence, stating Matteo Ginevra had attempted to prevent the two construction workers climbing aboard the girder. Both men were killed when the crane jammed and they fell fifty floors to the ground. Now back to the studio.'

Roscoe thumped his hand against the screen of the in-car TV.

Four days wasted in Chicago waiting to testify against Matteo Ginevra had been bad enough, but more than this he was incensed at the thought of a guilty man going free.

Jerry Davis was the third, and most crucial, of the prosecution witnesses to recant their evidence. Roscoe was in no doubt all three had been bought off – and that the Ginevra family fortune had cast a long shadow over the trial.

Two years earlier, as the recently appointed global head of security for Tribeca Luxury Hotels, a chain of the twenty-eight most exclusive hotels across the world, Roscoe had been in Chicago as a member of the team charged with developing the latest addition to the group's luxury portfolio.

With the hotel under construction in the city's downtown district, Roscoe had been responsible for the security structure in and around the hotel's core. Regularly home to some of the world's most powerful and influential people, all Tribeca Luxury Hotels were built with a security foundation that offered the greatest possible level of resistance to the terror threats in existence across the modern world.

That afternoon, as he walked from the hotel along the banks of the Chicago River, Roscoe had seen Matteo Ginevra drinking heavily in one of the newly opened riverside bars. Knowing Ginevra was heading up the Tribeca construction team, Roscoe had felt uncomfortable. But, telling himself Ginevra was the son of Enzo Ginevra and that the Ginevra Construction Group was one of the biggest global partners of Tribeca Luxury Hotels, he had convinced himself Matteo was finished for the day and walked on.

It was a moment's decision that had stayed with him every day for the next two years.

While Roscoe had sat and eaten lunch by the river, an intoxicated Ginevra had returned to the construction site. Surrounded by his entourage, he had started to goad two of the men working on the site. Relishing an opportunity to exhibit his power in front of his devotees, Matteo had bullied the two construction workers into riding unsecured up the outside of the new skyscraper.

The scene Roscoe had discovered when he returned an hour later was one he could still see each time he closed his eyes.

The mangled bodies of the two construction workers had lain shattered in pools of their own blood, having plunged over fifty floors onto the newly constructed sun terrace that overlooked the graceful river.

Now, watching the news report, his anger and frustration surfaced once more. In attempting to deliver a hotel that would provide the ultimate in security for its future guests, he had not provided that same security to the men charged with its construction.

He had failed them.

Listening to the end of the news report, he could still hear Matteo's voice from that tragic afternoon: 'Dead Hispanics are nothing more than a cost of doing business in the construction trade,' he had said to Roscoe as he walked away from the scene.

Roscoe wouldn't rest until Matteo Ginevra was behind bars.

WITH THE SNOW STILL falling, Roscoe's cab made its way round to the American Airlines terminal. His attention was drawn to a teenage girl hurtling out of the front of the building. With no regard for her own safety, she ran through the airport traffic, slamming her hand against the hood of Roscoe's car. Roscoe's driver jammed on his brakes and Roscoe was hurled forward against the cab's partition, only his outstretched arm breaking his fall.

And then, almost instantly, the cab was hit from behind. Roscoe was tossed forward, his head crashing into the divide.

'You okay back there?' said the driver as Roscoe, dazed and with a bloodied temple, pulled himself up off the floor.

'Fine,' said Roscoe, wiping away the blood from his forehead. He felt a pain rip through his right shoulder.

'Stupid kid,' said the driver. 'Gonna get herself killed if she don't watch where she's going.'

Roscoe looked out of his window at the girl, who continued to weave erratically through the traffic, now making her way across the elevated airport approach road.

'Cops coming after her,' said the driver. Roscoe turned to see two police officers exit the terminal building in pursuit of the girl. 'Maybe she's one of those Islam terror women, beholden to their menfolk. She can be beholden to me any time she likes,' he added, laughing to himself.

The driver's last comment was lost on Roscoe, who was already opening his door. Car horns blared and frustrated drivers shouted at the stacked-up vehicles around them, as he ducked through the traffic in pursuit of the girl.

'Hold up!' he called as she ran towards the edge of the elevated road. 'Please, wait!' he shouted. He glanced behind to see the two police officers now with their weapons drawn. With more snow now lying on the ground, he saw one of the officers take a Bambie-style slide across the road, his feet suddenly flying above his head. Car horns sounded with greater intensity in apparent celebration of the officer's undignified fall.

The girl was running across the rail track that encircled the airport to ferry passengers from terminal to terminal. Roscoe doubled his pace.

'Stop! Let me help you,' he shouted again.

The girl turned and looked over her shoulder. Roscoe could see genuine fear etched into her young face.

But she did not stop.

Instead he could only watch as the girl climbed the barrier that edged the elevated road so that she was standing precariously on the concrete ledge.

Roscoe slowed to a stop.

The girl was staring down at a hundred-foot drop below.

'COME AWAY FROM THE edge,' Roscoe pleaded, fearful his voice would be drowned out by the deafening engines of a departing plane, soaring above them.

Blinded by the snow, he moved closer. He could just see the girl's bleached-blonde hair, much of it tucked beneath a Chicago Bears cap, contrasting with her dark, Mediterranean skin. She half turned to look at him and he caught sight of the desperation in her deep brown eyes.

Quickly, she turned back and edged forward to the drop.

'Wait!' called Roscoe, pushing his sodden blonde hair back from his forehead. Looking round, he could see the police officers quickly coming up behind him. Knowing they would only succeed in spooking the girl further, he turned and held up his hands, showing them he was unarmed.

The officers slowed and Roscoe turned back to the girl.

'What's your name?' he called to her, realising the need to engage her in conversation. 'Mine's Jon, and I'm starting to wish I'd grabbed my jacket before I ran after you.'

JAMES PATTERSON BOOKSHOTS

COMING SOON

HIDDEN

Rejected by the Navy SEALs, Mitchum is content to be his small town's unofficial private eye, until his beloved 14-year-old cousin is abducted. Now he'll call on every lethal skill to track her down . . .

THE HOUSE HUSBAND

Detective Teaghan Beaumont is getting closer and closer to discovering the truth about Darien Marshall. But there's a twist that she – and you, dear reader – will never see coming.

EXQUISITE: THE DIAMOND TRILOGY, PART 3

Siobhan and Derick's relationship has been a rollercoaster ride that has pushed Derick too far. Will Siobhan be able to win back her soul mate?

KISSES AT MIDNIGHT

Three exciting romances – *The McCullagh Inn in Maine*, *Sacking the Quarterback* and *Seducing Shakespeare*.

SEDUCING SHAKESPEARE (ebook only)

William Shakespeare has fallen in love – with the beautiful Marietta DiSonna. But what Shakespeare doesn't know is that Marietta is acting a role. Unless Shakespeare can seduce her in return . . .

ALSO BY JAMES PATTERSON

ALEX CROSS NOVELS

Along Came a Spider
Kiss the Girls
Jack and Jill
Cat and Mouse
Pop Goes the Weasel
Roses are Red
Violets are Blue
Four Blind Mice
The Big Bad Wolf
London Bridges
Mary, Mary
Cross
Double Cross
Cross Country
Alex Cross's Trial (*with Richard DiLallo*)
I, Alex Cross
Cross Fire
Kill Alex Cross
Merry Christmas, Alex Cross
Alex Cross, Run
Cross My Heart
Hope to Die
Cross Justice
Cross the Line

THE WOMEN'S MURDER CLUB SERIES

1st to Die
2nd Chance (*with Andrew Gross*)
3rd Degree (*with Andrew Gross*)
4th of July (*with Maxine Paetro*)
The 5th Horseman (*with Maxine Paetro*)
The 6th Target (*with Maxine Paetro*)
7th Heaven (*with Maxine Paetro*)
8th Confession (*with Maxine Paetro*)
9th Judgement (*with Maxine Paetro*)
10th Anniversary (*with Maxine Paetro*)
11th Hour (*with Maxine Paetro*)
12th of Never (*with Maxine Paetro*)
Unlucky 13 (*with Maxine Paetro*)
14th Deadly Sin (*with Maxine Paetro*)
15th Affair (*with Maxine Paetro*)

DETECTIVE MICHAEL BENNETT SERIES

Step on a Crack (*with Michael Ledwidge*)
Run for Your Life (*with Michael Ledwidge*)
Worst Case (*with Michael Ledwidge*)
Tick Tock (*with Michael Ledwidge*)
I, Michael Bennett (*with Michael Ledwidge*)
Gone (*with Michael Ledwidge*)
Burn (*with Michael Ledwidge*)
Alert (*with Michael Ledwidge*)
Bullseye (*with Michael Ledwidge*)

PRIVATE NOVELS

Private (*with Maxine Paetro)*
Private London (*with Mark Pearson*)
Private Games (*with Mark Sullivan*)
Private: No. 1 Suspect (*with Maxine Paetro*)
Private Berlin (*with Mark Sullivan*)

Private Down Under (*with Michael White*)
Private L.A. (*with Mark Sullivan*)
Private India (*with Ashwin Sanghi*)
Private Vegas (*with Maxine Paetro*)
Private Sydney (*with Kathryn Fox*)
Private Paris (*with Mark Sullivan*)
The Games (*with Mark Sullivan*)

NYPD RED SERIES

NYPD Red (*with Marshall Karp*)
NYPD Red 2 (*with Marshall Karp*)
NYPD Red 3 (*with Marshall Karp*)
NYPD Red 4 (*with Marshall Karp*)

STAND-ALONE THRILLERS

Sail (*with Howard Roughan*)
Swimsuit (*with Maxine Paetro*)
Don't Blink (*with Howard Roughan*)
Postcard Killers (*with Liza Marklund*)
Toys (*with Neil McMahon*)
Now You See Her (*with Michael Ledwidge*)
Kill Me If You Can (*with Marshall Karp*)
Guilty Wives (*with David Ellis*)
Zoo (*with Michael Ledwidge*)
Second Honeymoon (*with Howard Roughan*)
Mistress (*with David Ellis*)
Invisible (*with David Ellis*)
The Thomas Berryman Number
Truth or Die (*with Howard Roughan*)
Murder House (*with David Ellis*)
Never Never (*with Candice Fox*)
Woman of God (*with Maxine Paetro*)

BOOKSHOTS

Black & Blue (*with Candice Fox*)
Break Point (*with Lee Stone*)
Cross Kill
Private Royals (*with Rees Jones*)
The Hostage (*with Robert Gold*)
Zoo 2 (*with Max DiLallo*)
Heist (*with Rees Jones*)
Hunted (*with Andrew Holmes*)
Airport: Code Red (*with Michael White*)
The Trial (*with Maxine Paetro*)
Little Black Dress (*with Emily Raymond*)
Chase (*with Michael Ledwidge*)
Let's Play Make-Believe (*with James O. Born*)
Dead Heat (*with Lee Stone*)
Triple Threat
113 Minutes (*with Max DiLallo*)
The Verdict (*with Robert Gold*)
French Kiss (*with Richard DiLallo*)
$10,000,000 Marriage Proposal (*with Hilary Liftin*)
Kill or Be Killed
Taking the Titanic (*with Scott Slaven*)
Killer Chef (*with Jeffrey J. Keyes*)